THE BLITZ BUS

Glen Blackwell

Cover illustration by Vera Egoshina

Zoetrope Books

Published by Zoetrope Books 2021
Suffolk, England

A CIP catalogue record for this book is available from the
British Library

ISBN : 978-1-8383252-2-0

www.zoetropebooks.com

For Dad

Thank you for inspiring me

Catching The Bus

Jack stared out of the window as he tapped his pen against the flecked top of the desk. The sun was streaming in through the glass and making him feel sleepy. It had been a long day and he wasn't finding the English lesson very interesting. The class had been asked to write a fictional diary entry for a Second World War evacuee and Jack was finding it hard to get started. The teacher had begun the lesson by showing some black and white photos of children waiting to board trains to take them out of London to relative safety in the countryside. She had asked the class to consider how those children might have felt - being away from family and friends for possibly the first time - and write about it.

"Jack," said the teacher, Mrs Carson, "are you planning to write anything today, or just stare out of the window?"

"Sorry, Miss," replied Jack, "I was trying to imagine how different it must have looked all those years ago."

"Well, you've only got 10 minutes left and I'd like at least a side of paper," Mrs Carson reminded him.

Jack's gaze flicked back to the window. He'd lived in East London his whole life and, despite the city constantly changing around him, he was finding it hard to imagine what it must have been like in wartime. He was 12, and in his first year at high school – his main interests were football and video games, and the Second World War seemed a long way away from the classroom on that afternoon.

They had learned in a history lesson about the bombing raids on London which were referred to as the Blitz and Jack knew that some of the modern buildings he could see would have been built to replace bomb damaged houses. The school was in a mostly residential area, surrounded by houses and flats, and he supposed that a lot of people locally would have been impacted by having their homes damaged or destroyed. He tried to imagine what it might be like if a bomb fell on his house. "Boom!" he said quietly to himself, but it didn't help – the thought of his cosy modern life being literally thrown up in the air was incomprehensible.

He struggled through a couple of paragraphs of writing, trying to draw on how he thought he might feel about seeing his local area slip away past the windows of a train. He definitely wasn't feeling the lesson though – he very much needed a topic bringing to life in order to fully understand it.

As the bell for the end of the lesson rang, and the

rest of the class started packing up their things, Jack hurriedly scribbled a third paragraph before getting up and dropping his paper in the tray on Mrs Carson's desk. He went back to collect his bag and then joined the queue of students filing out of the classroom into the wide corridor.

"Jack – wait a minute please," Mrs Carson called. He groaned inwardly.

"Yes, Miss?"

"This isn't good enough. I asked for at least a side and you've done half that at best. Sit back down and have another go."

Jack reached for his paper from the tray. "No," Mrs Carson instructed, "there's barely anything on it – start again and give me two sides this time please."

Scowling, Jack made his way back to the desk he'd been sitting at and sat down. He took out a pen and his pad of paper and tried to recall what he'd written initially. The minutes ticked by as he struggled to focus, regretting not paying more attention to the start of the lesson. Then it hit him – he'd agreed to meet Emmie after school – they were going to hang out in one of the local parks. He put his head in his hands – he was never going to make it on time without some serious inspiration.

Emmeline Langford – or Emmie to her friends – was having a bit more success in her lesson. She was in a different stream to Jack and this afternoon her class were doing drama. The theme for their year group this term was the Second World War and it had been woven into many of the subjects. In drama, the students had been asked to act out how they thought the conversation might go between parents and their children who were being evacuated. The drama teacher had chosen not to show any historical material, but instead asked that the class thought about how they might feel in the same situation and act out the first things which came into their heads.

Emmie sat back, idly twirling one of her dark plaits, as she watched another group of girls go first. There was a lot of focus in their performance around how sad the parents were but how excited for adventure the children were feeling. Emmie wondered if she would feel excited in the same situation or nervous about so much change.

Mr Foxton, the drama teacher, was clearly very impressed by the first group's performance and clapped as they finished and returned to their seats.

"No pressure then," muttered Emmie to her friend Claire, who she was sitting next to. "Shall we go next and get it over with?" Claire nodded her agreement. She was a slender girl, with a serious face, and acting didn't come as easily to her as it did to Emmie.

As the girls got up and walked to the front of the room, along with two more of their classmates, Emmie could feel some emotion rising inside her. It really must have been very scary to leave all you knew behind and journey off into the unknown.

Their performance was quite different to the first group – the girls knew each other well and were able to improvise, based on what was being said. Emmie played the role of the mother, trying to reassure her children that they would be safer going to the countryside, despite not being totally convinced it was the right thing to do.

There was a pause as they finished, and Emmie wondered what was coming next, before the entire class broke out into spontaneous applause. "Well done - there was so much feeling in that narrative," complimented Mr Foxton, as they sat down. Emmie smiled – she found it much easier to interpret a situation if she imagined herself in it first.

After the rest of the groups had performed, their homework sheets were handed out. They were asked to find a film to watch featuring the Second World War, and then write about how one of the actors might have got themselves into character. There was a list of suggested films – some older and others more modern.

As the lesson ended, Claire turned to Emmie. "What are you doing after school?" she asked. "Do you want to come back to mine and we can check some of these films out?"

"Thanks, but maybe another day?" Emmie replied, "I said I'd meet Jack at the bus stop today."

"Yeah, ok – later in the week then?" Claire suggested. At their old school, there had only been one set of classes in each year, but the high school split students into two streams, each then having lessons at different times of the week. It made it hard to see friends in the other stream except at lunchtime or after school.

Emmie swung her bag onto her shoulder and walked out of the drama studio with Claire. They chatted as they walked into the fresh air and around the back of the building, heading for the main playground at the front of the school.

As they walked through the gate together and out onto the pavement, Emmie asked, "How did you feel about that drama lesson then?"

"What do you mean?" Claire replied.

"Well, the part about imagining being separated from your family."

"It was quite tough to know what to say at first," admitted Claire. "How about you?"

"I find I need to imagine myself in a similar situation, but one that's relatable to me," Emmie explained. "If I think, for example, about going on a week's school trip for the first time and whether I'd be nervous or excited."

"Makes sense," Claire agreed. "Where did you say you were meeting Jack?" They had reached the bus stop on the corner of the main road.

"Here," Emmie answered, looking at her watch, "five minutes ago."

"I hope he hasn't stood you up."

"He wouldn't dare," laughed Emmie, feeling a little less confident than she sounded.

"Ok, well see you tomorrow then." Claire waved as she crossed the road, heading home and Emmie joined the queue at the bus stop. There was already a crowd of pupils from their school waiting for the bus, and the first one which came into sight didn't even stop as it was so full.

Emmie looked at her watch again – maybe Jack had stood her up? After about 15 minutes and two buses had passed, she was at the front of the queue and saw a red, double decker bus inching its way through the traffic along the road. It was decision time now – should she get on the bus or not?

He's not coming, she decided, stepping forward and onto the bus as it came to a halt. She walked between the seats, slipping into one on the pavement side. She put her bag down by her feet and then looked up, only to see a tall, orange haired boy running towards the bus stop and looking desperately around. She banged on the window and waved frantically at him, at the same time hearing the fateful hiss of the driver operating the doors. It seemed like Jack had heard it too and put on an extra burst of speed.

"Wait please!" called Emmie, in the direction of the driver, who was already releasing the brake and moving away from the kerb. There was no reply and Emmie slumped down in her seat, frustrated at the way the afternoon had turned out.

Lights, Camera, Action!

"Shall we go through the Gardens on the way home?" Emmie felt a tap on her shoulder and turned to see Jack grinning at her. "Come on, it'll be fun – we can even get some chips."

"Ok," replied Emmie as she stretched in her seat. "You're buying though!" She grinned back, her braces sparkling, "How did you get onto the bus after the driver shut the doors?"

He ran his hand through his short hair, looking pleased with himself. "Nipped on at the back step. Easy."

The bus rumbled on down Bethnal Green Road. It was early October – the kind of day where the warmth of summer could still be felt when the sun came out from behind a cloud. The traffic was heavy and their journey from school had been stop-start all the way. It would be nice to sit on a bench in the Gardens and talk about the day.

Jack breathed out onto the window and then idly traced a figure in the condensation with his finger. The bus ride was always so dull – now they were at high school and couldn't walk home, it meant a crawling, crowded existence instead. He looked at his watch – 4:35 but it felt later, as clouds started to darken the sky.

As the bus slowed down ahead of the railway bridge, Emmie turned around. "Chips then, Jack?" As he opened his mouth to reply, she grabbed her bag, jumped up from her seat and walked down the aisle, dark plaits swinging behind her.

Jack caught her up and peered out of the window. They were standing just behind the driver, waiting for the bus to come to a stop. "Look there," he pointed, "that's one of those funny gas masks from the history lesson last week. Did you see that video too?"

Emmie looked up and saw Jack was gesturing towards a blue-painted shop with a mannequin in the window. The mannequin was wearing a long, dark coat and it did indeed have a gas mask over its face. "How strange – I've never seen that shop before," said Emmie. "We come along here every day and it definitely wasn't there yesterday." She looked thoughtful – trying to search her memory for any clues and then giving up. "I wonder why the window's set up like that – there doesn't seem to be anything else there at all. Come on – let's have a look."

The bus pulled up at the stop and Emmie stepped down onto the pavement. As Jack put his feet down onto the ground, suddenly there was a blinding flash and the earth seemed to shake. He grabbed Emmie with one hand and a lamppost with the other. "What was that?!" he stuttered, his legs shaking. Emmie hung onto his arm and steadied herself too.

As she looked around, everyone else on the street seemed to be behaving perfectly normally and as if they were totally unaware of what had just happened. The bus pulled away and Emmie looked at it in surprise - seeing the unusual sight of a conductor standing on the back step. She blinked and rubbed her eyes but, at the same moment, it started to rain heavily.

"Come on Emmie, let's shelter in the Tube," suggested Jack, pulling his school blazer tightly around him. They giggled as they ran along the pavement, arm in arm, dodging the other pedestrians - most of whom were frantically trying to open umbrellas. Emmie noticed that almost all of the men they passed were wearing hats. "Quick, the lights are red, let's cross," Jack tugged her arm as they made their way across the road, in front of a stationary bus. Something felt a little odd, but the rain was streaming down their faces so hard that Emmie put it to the back of her mind and carried on.

They reached the steps of the Tube station and clattered down, a mournful wail drifting after them, followed by a lot of shouting. As they reached the bottom of the steps and stopped to take a breath,

Emmie looked around. This was definitely odd – the posters on the wall were really old fashioned and everyone seemed to be dressed quite formally – most of the men wore suits and the women were largely wearing dresses.

"No chips then, I guess?" said Jack, looking disappointed. "I don't fancy getting any wetter though." He turned his head to look at Emmie – "Are you ok?" he asked, "you look like you've seen a ghost."

Emmie didn't get a chance to answer as, at that moment, a large crowd of people started coming down the stairs into the booking hall. "Move on down to the platforms," said a man with an official sounding voice. Emmie and Jack got swept along in the throng, moving swiftly toward the escalators and then down to the platform level.

As they turned the corner onto the platform, both Jack and Emmie stopped in surprise – where there were usually people sat on benches, waiting for a train, there now stood rows and rows of bunk beds! There were even bunks down where the track should be. "What's going on?" Emmie whispered quietly, "is everyone in fancy dress?"

Jack, still thinking about his chips, looked around. "Maybe there's some kind of event going on?"

"Move along, please!" a man in a white tin helmet said loudly. Emmie looked at him curiously, and found her feet moving forward again, along with the rest of the crowd.

"Let's sit down over here," suggested Jack. They sank gratefully onto one of the lower bunks and stared at the mass of people slowly filing past, most talking quietly and taking their places on the bunks around them.

"What's going on?" Emmie said again – this time her voice wavering slightly. "Do you think this is some sort of film set? Have they closed the station for the day?"

"Cool!" replied Jack, "maybe we'll get to be in a film?" He looked around – there were still people coming onto the platform and almost all of the bunks were full now. There were a group of young children just along from where they sat who were playing a game of marbles on the platform edge – every so often a marble would roll off and someone in the track area would hand it back to them.

"I don't like this – I think we should get going." Emmie tugged on Jack's arm - "There's something not quite right going on." She stood, picking up her school bag in one hand. Suddenly, 'RUR, RUR, RUR, RUR' - there was a series of muffled vibrations from above their heads. Emmie's eyes bulged – "Now, Jack! Come on."

"It's only a train going through on the other track,"

Jack said, surprised. He got up anyway and slowly followed Emmie back along the platform and through to the base of the escalators. There were people everywhere, some had spread blankets out on the floor, and there was a low murmur of conversation. Jack led the way up the central stairs again as the escalators still weren't moving. It was hard going as there were people sat all the way up the staircase on one side.

As they reached the top and found themselves back in the ticket hall, there was another dull noise – this time it sounded more like a 'CRUUUMMMPPP'. "That's not a train!" shouted Emmie, quickening her pace towards the exit. As they turned to go up the final steps, they were met by a metal gate and a burly policeman with a tall helmet and bright buttons on his tunic.

"You can't go out there, Miss," he said firmly. "It's not safe."

"What do you mean? I want to go home!" cried Emmie. She grabbed at the gate and shook it, but it was locked shut.

"Please, we just want to leave," pleaded Jack. "This is all very realistic, but we'll be late home for tea if we don't go now."

"Realistic? What on earth do you mean?" asked the policeman. "There's an air raid going on out there and the bombs won't care if you're late or not!"

"This is a film set, right?" replied Jack. "We didn't know they were shooting anything down here, otherwise we'd have stayed away. We only came in because it was raining."

The policeman stared incredulously at Jack – "Are you kidding?" he said, "the whole German air force is up there dropping bombs, and you're cracking jokes."

Emmie rattled the gate again – "Come on Jack," she begged. "Please," she turned to the policeman, "just let us go home."

"That's it, I've had enough! You'd better scoot or you'll be in big trouble. Go on – now, or you'll be spending a night in the cells!" The policeman took a step towards them, and both Jack and Emmie turned and ran back to the escalators. They stumbled down onto the platform again, through the rows of people lining every bit of available space.

Emmie turned to Jack with tears in her eyes – "What's happening to us? Where are we?" He hugged her close to him.

"I… I don't know anymore…" he stuttered. "It's a very realistic film set – what else can it be?"

Emmie let out a huge sob – "It's not a film set," she cried. She held onto Jack for a moment, then took a step back, closed her eyes and shouted, "WHERE AM I?"

"Bethnal Green Tube, love," came a voice from behind her. "I know it might be hard to believe, but they finally got around to building a station here. I mean, it's only 1940 after all!"

"1940?" breathed Emmie, "how on earth...."

"Maybe we've stepped back in time," Jack suggested, not really meaning it.

She stared at him, a look of horror on her face. Her heart was pounding, and she was finding it hard to hold back her tears. As Jack tried to put a comforting arm around her again, she could feel a tremor and realised that he was shaking too.

3

Conkers & Potato Pie

It was cold in the bedroom. A grey light was visible through the curtains, and Jan wriggled down a bit further under his blanket, trying to work out how to avoid getting out of bed. He heard a creak on the stairs – "Come on Jan, breakfast is ready."

Jan swung his legs out of bed, felt his feet touch the rug and then stood up. He dressed quickly, pulling on his long shorts, thick woollen socks, shirt and pullover. He made his way downstairs to the kitchen, where Mama was making toast on the range. She was a short woman, with dark curly hair and a shy smile. She wasn't his real mother of course - he had left her behind in Danzig last summer when he was sent away to safety in England with so many other children, just prior to the war starting. He closed his eyes for a moment and recalled the long train journey, followed by a bumpy sea crossing and another train journey, which had finally seen him living with Mrs Tubbs and her elderly father. Mrs Tubbs didn't have any children of her own and liked being called Mama – it didn't matter either way to Jan, who was just grateful for the relative safety of wartime London.

"Would you like some dripping on your toast, Jan?" Mama asked. She was holding out a plate with two slices of toast in one hand and a brown earthenware jar in the other.

"Yes please," replied Jan. He had grown used to this strange, spreadable fat over the past year in England. It didn't taste anywhere near as good as butter but was a lot better than dry toast. As Jan ate, the door opened, and he looked up.

"Morning, young Jan," said a cheery voice. Old Mr Tubbs entered the room, shuffling slightly. He was a white haired, softly spoken man who often suffered with a bad back. "I've just been out to feed the chickens," he announced. The Tubbs family kept 3 chickens in the small, paved back yard to provide them with fresh eggs. There wasn't much space in the yard and the chicken coop meant that Jan had to go to the nearby Bethnal Green Gardens if he wanted to play.

Mr Tubbs sat down and poured himself a cup of tea. "You'll have to hurry up if you want to get to school on time," he observed.

Jan finished his toast and a glass of water, then headed outside to the toilet in the yard. Sheets of yesterday's newspaper were hanging up on a nail, and Jan idly gazed at them as he sat on the seat. The main story was about the RAF conducting the heaviest

bombing raid on Berlin to date. Jan shuddered a bit –
if living through that was anything like the nightly
experience in London, then it wouldn't be fun at all.

He headed back inside, picked up his gas mask and
said goodbye to Mama. Mr Tubbs had disappeared
again by that point. "Be good, Jan," she instructed him,
as he closed the front door.

School was a strange, formal experience compared
to his life in Poland. There, the class had sat around the
teacher in a group and been encouraged to discuss
what they were learning – completely different to the
authoritarian English approach in 1940. A lot of the
children had been evacuated to the countryside and
the younger male teachers had been called up to fight.
The remaining staff were very strict on discipline and
hated anyone being late. Jan often had to run through
the streets to school, his gas mask box banging on his
back as he did so.

Once at school, Jan took his place in the classroom
– he sat at the end of a long row of wooden desks,
facing a blackboard. One of the other boys was ink
monitor that day and was already walking round filling
up the inkwells on each desk. Jan found the
schoolwork quite easy but still struggled with writing
the language. He had learned English at his school in
Poland and was conversationally fluent but found
writing a lot of the words that his classmates and the

teachers used was difficult.

"Good morning class," boomed the teacher, as he entered the room. The children all quickly stood up behind their desks and returned the greeting. "You may sit," he continued.

The first lesson was geography and, as the teacher pinned up a map of the British Empire, with large swathes of the world coloured red, Jan couldn't help thinking of the irony. Here they were, learning how 'Great' Great Britain was, yet another world order was flexing its muscles just across the English Channel. He doubted that many of the others in the class would feel this way, but they had not yet seen their country as directly threatened as he had.

Break time came, and Jan found himself involved in a game of conkers. There was a large horse chestnut tree in the corner of the playground and every autumn it disgorged several weeks-worth of fun for the whole school. Last year, when Jan had first arrived at the school, he had been thoroughly confused at this game of hitting one chestnut with another, but now was becoming something of a master at it.

"Go Jan, go Jan," called a group of girls from behind him. He was representing his class in an unofficial tournament and it was currently tied – 3 apiece. He took a step back, then brought his conker down smartly on the one held by Davy Brown from Class 8. Nothing, not even a crack. It was Davy's turn now – he smiled a thin smile and hit Jan's conker squarely on the top. Before Jan's eyes, his conker disintegrated, and he was left holding the shoelace which it had been threaded onto.

"How did you do that?!" asked Jan in surprise.

"Vinegar," came the reply. "I boiled it in vinegar overnight – toughens them right up."

The children watching the conker game drifted away, leaving Jan on his own once again. He had struggled to make friends since arriving, despite spending a whole school year in London. The class was quite small, and everyone seemed to have formed their own friendship groups already. Jan smiled sadly to himself, recalling the boys he used to play with back in Danzig. He wondered where they all were now and felt a few tears welling up inside him.

Before his thoughts could wander any further, a teacher appeared, ringing a bell to signify the end of break time. Everyone lined up in rows and marched back into their classrooms in turn. The rest of the day was taken up with maths and English, and Jan was relieved when the final bell rang, telling them it was time to go home.

That evening, tea was rather uninspiring. Mama had been to the butchers and queued for ages, only to find that they had run out of everything by the time she got near to the front. Instead, she had made a vegetable pie with potato pastry.

"What do you think, Jan?" she asked. "I got the recipe from a lady in the butchers queue."

"It's… interesting," replied Jan. "I like the bright colours of the vegetables."

Mr Tubbs threw back his head and roared with laughter. "Even after a year, you're still so polite, Jan!" He continued chuckling as Jan and Mama finished off their pie.

"Would you like to know what's for pudding?" Mama asked. When Jan nodded, she carried on – "Steamed chocolate sponge."

"Probably made of potato too," said Mr Tubbs, winking at Jan.

"Well yes, it is I'm afraid," replied Mama. "You should be used to the rationing by now – it's hard to be creative when there's not a lot of variety. Try it though – you might like it."

Just then, the air raid sirens wailed – no one was going to get any pudding tonight. Mama looked at Mr Tubbs – "Should we go to the shelter?" she asked. The authorities had constructed a brick air raid shelter at the end of their street earlier that summer, in the expectation of bombing raids. It was an ugly, square structure, built on a wide part of the pavement, with wooden benches lining each wall inside. No-one liked going to it and consequently it was barely ever full.

"I'm not sitting in that horrible, damp street shelter," he replied. "It plays havoc with my back. We'll go to the Tube station instead."

"Are you sure?" said Mama. The station had been built a year earlier, but the line had yet to be extended to reach it, and local people had taken to sheltering there during bombing raids. "I know people try to use it but there are all of those posters outside warning not to."

"Well, it's not damp, so that's where I'm going," announced Mr Tubbs, standing up and reaching for his coat.

"Come on then, Jan. Guess we're going there too," Mama told him.

Jan put on his overcoat and slung his gas mask over his shoulder. Everyone was meant to carry them, in case of a gas attack, though many people had started to ignore the advice. Mama was a stickler for the rules and insisted Jan carried it wherever he went. It was annoying at times but had become as much a part of his life as pulling a coat on when he left the house now.

They left the house and quickly walked along the twilight roads towards the Tube station entrance. The blackout meant that once it got dark, it got really dark – there were even white lines painted on the kerb to stop people accidentally wandering into the road.

Once they arrived at the station, they joined the slow queue of people shuffling through the entrance and down the stairs. There was a policeman standing at the top, as if to deter people from coming in, but he didn't say anything to them as they passed. They walked down the central stairs to the platform and looked for some bunks to sit on. It was already filling up and there was a steady flow of people coming in.

Jan sat down on a bunk next to Mama and gazed around. There was a family next to them with 2 small girls tucked into a bunk together, and a group of older men trying to have a singsong on the bunks that faced them on the track bed. Suddenly, Jan heard a commotion further along the tunnel - a girl with dark plaits was shouting and a boy was trying to comfort her. The girl seemed really distressed and wouldn't stop crying. Jan wondered where their mother was – families tended to come to the shelters together.

After a while, he turned away, not wanting to stare. He lay down on his side of the bunk and tried to get some sleep – it was likely to be a long night.

Unexploded Bomb

Emmie opened her eyes a crack – she had the uneasy feeling that often came after a bad dream, but this wasn't a bad dream, was it? In the end, they'd given up trying to understand what had happened last night and tried to sleep. Jack had joked about time travel – neither of them believing it to be a realistic explanation – but this morning it felt somehow more plausible. She looked around and could see the rows of bunks stretching the length of the platform, with people quietly collecting their things and then filing towards the exit. She heard a creak from above – Jack must be awake too.

"Jack," she said quietly, "are you awake?" There was a murmur in response – Jack wasn't a morning person. Emmie reached up and poked the underneath of the mattress above her. "Jack!" she said again, more urgently this time.

After a bit more shuffling, Jack's head appeared over the edge of the bunk. "Uh, hi Emmie, what's up?" he asked.

"Well, in case you'd forgotten, we seem to be stuck

somewhere quite weird," Emmie whispered, trying not to be heard by the lady in the next bunk. "I think we should get out of here – everyone seems to be allowed to leave now anyway."

Jack's head disappeared and was replaced by his legs dangling over the side of the bunk. He jumped to the ground and tucked his crumpled shirt back into his trousers. "That was a bit intense last night – when the policeman wouldn't let us out, wasn't it?" He bent to tie a shoelace, looking up at Emmie suddenly as a realisation hit him – "This can't be a film set," he said quietly.

"Why not?" answered Emmie, though she was fairly sure that she agreed.

"There's no cameras or crew – in fact, there's nothing but people dressed in old clothes and acting a bit strangely." He finished tying his lace and sat on the end of Emmie's bunk. "I can't explain the missing rails either – how would a film crew be allowed to do something like that?"

"I think you're right," Emmie said slowly – speaking at a more normal volume now the bunks around them had emptied. "Shall we go outside and see if we can be certain? Maybe we can find some food too – I'm starving."

They picked up their school bags and joined the queue of people on the platform edge. Slowly, they made their way back to the escalators and then up the central stairs. "It's a shame the escalators aren't working," said Jack, "all these stairs to climb instead..."

"The station doesn't feel finished, does it?" offered Emmie. "That woman last night said something about it being new in 1940. I wonder if the escalators have ever worked..." Soon, they were at the top and made their way out of the exit, past the gate which had been so firmly shut last night. They emerged, blinking, into the brightening sky of an early autumn morning.

"Look - over there," said Jack, pointing, "looks like some sort of takeaway van." Across the path, just inside the entrance to the Gardens, was a green painted van with a window in the side and a queue of people forming. "Let's see if we can get something to eat," he suggested.

As they approached the van, they could smell food cooking and saw there was a chalk board listing what was on offer. It mainly seemed to be soup and bread. "What's 'WVS'?" asked Emmie, looking at the side of the van.

"Not sure," replied Jack, "but food's food." As they moved forward in the queue, they noticed that no-one seemed to be paying. "It must be some kind of charity food stall," Jack said to Emmie. As they approached the window, an old man in front of them was taking a big mug of steaming soup. "Three cheers for the Women's Voluntary Service," he said, raising the mug.

"Ah, so that's what 'WVS' stands for," Emmie nudged Jack. It was their turn and, as they gratefully took the soup and slices of bread offered, Emmie noticed a sign behind the counter - 'Helping Bombed Out Londoners'. "I feel a bit of a fraud – they're trying to help people with nothing," she said as they walked away.

Jack hungrily ate his bread – "We've got nothing right now either, Emmie." They walked further into the Gardens and both stopped in surprise again. Where there used to be grass was now entirely turned over to growing vegetables. "This is like a giant allotment," Jack said. "Didn't we learn about this in history? People turning their gardens over to growing food?"

"Dig for victory," Emmie replied. She was looking at a poster on the low fence which ran around the edge of the plot. It showed a foot pressing a spade into the soil, with the bold headline in red and white. They sat down on a bench to finish their soup and work out what to do next.

"I'm still not sure exactly what's going on," said Jack after a while. "I mean, this is all very realistic, but time travel…? It's just not possible, is it?" He looked around – there were birds singing in the trees and the gentle rumble of traffic from the road outside. It all seemed so, well, normal.

"Let's go back to the bus stop," suggested Emmie.

"It all started to get a bit strange when we got off the bus yesterday – maybe by going back, we can work out what's going on?"

"Ok," Jack agreed, drinking the last of his soup. "Let's take these mugs back on the way." They walked back to the Gardens entrance, placed their mugs on a table alongside the WVS van and turned left onto the pavement outside.

As they rounded the next corner and came back to the railway bridge near the bus stop, they stopped again – this time more in shock than surprise. Next to the pub, a whole row of buildings had disappeared and there was a large pile of rubble in their place, spilling out into the road. Further along, a policeman stood in front of a wooden barrier, preventing any traffic from passing. There was a hastily-painted sign on the barrier which read 'DANGER – UNEXPLODED BOMB'.

"The paper shop and the drycleaners – where have they gone?" murmured Emmie, her face white as a sheet. "I was only there yesterday..." She turned to Jack, tears pricking at her eyes and could see that he was upset too. "This must be real – no-one could make up something so realistic in a big city overnight." They crossed the road to look closer and were both surprised to see that there was no fencing or barrier of any kind along the pavement – just rubble in big mounds scattered everywhere. They watched a few people picking their way through the destruction, seemingly undeterred by their surroundings.

"I guess there's no Health and Safety in 1940," said Jack, with half a smile. He was trying to lighten the mood but they both felt really low now. It had seemed impossible that they had slipped back in time but the evidence in front of them was overwhelming.

"I can't believe people live like this," said Emmie quietly, "they're being so normal, yet this is totally not normal."

"We've got to get home," Jack said with determination, putting his hand into Emmie's. "Let's go back to the bus stop like you said."

"We can't go down there though," Emmie pointed at the pile of rubble in front of the railway bridge. "Maybe we could go round somehow – come at the bus stop from the other direction?"

"Do you think it's that bus stop specifically, or just a bus, which is the key to this?" Jack was trying to replay the events of the past afternoon in his head. "Or it might be something to do with that funny shop which we saw – you know, the one which you didn't think was there before...?"

"When we were on the bus it was normal," said Emmie, also trying to recall exactly what had happened when. "It was when we got off that something had changed." She had a fleeting memory of running in the rain and noticing that people were dressed slightly differently to normal.

"Well, we just need a bus then," decided Jack. "We can't go down there, so why not go to the next stop along and jump on the first bus home?" He sounded convinced by his idea, even if he wasn't totally trusting of any of his senses today.

"Ok," Emmie agreed, and they turned around and headed for the next bus stop – this one was parallel to the Gardens. There was no-one at the bus stop, just a post with the route numbers showing. "Number 8 still stops here," Emmie said with some relief. Buses were usually every 6 minutes, but it would be interesting to see how frequent they were in 1940...

After 20 minutes, they were almost giving up hope when a red double decker bus trundled into view, covered in advertising boards. Jack put his arm out and the bus slowed to a halt. They both jumped onto the back step and threw themselves into the first empty seat.

"Tickets please," came the voice of the conductor from behind them as the bus started to move off. Jack put his hand into his pocket for some change and held it out.

"Two please – to town," he said, handing over the coins.

"What's this then?" asked the conductor. "Funny

31

money? You can't pay with that."

Jack looked down at the outstretched hand. "We don't have any old money," he muttered to Emmie. Then he looked up at the conductor – "Please. You see, we've..."

"I don't want to hear it, sonny," said the conductor sternly. "You pay or you get off."

Jack looked at Emmie, who slowly shook her head. "We'll get off," he mumbled, tears pricking at his eyes for the second time that morning. They stood up and waited by the back step as the bus passed the junction covered in rubble and took a detour down the next street – the conductor glaring at them the whole time. As the bus slowed, they stepped off and began to retrace their steps.

"How are we going to get back if we can't even get on a bus?" wondered Emmie out loud. "Seems like it's not as easy to time travel as it might appear..."

"Let's walk around and see what we can find," suggested Jack. "If we're stuck here then we need to work out how to eat and where to sleep."

"I think we'll be back in the Tube station later," replied Emmie. "It was dry and fairly comfortable at least. We could definitely do with finding somewhere to eat though..."

As they crossed the road again by the pub, a policeman called – "Oi! Why aren't you at school?" He walked purposefully towards them. Jack and Emmie both looked around – the pavement was quite full of people now and they were just by the entrance to the Gardens.

"Run!" shouted Jack, sensing something wasn't right. He tugged Emmie's arm and pulled her in the direction of the Gardens. The policeman started to run after them. Jack dodged around a hedge, Emmie close behind, then they sprinted along the side of the vegetable plot before Jack pulled them behind a large rhododendron bush. "Down!" he hissed, motioning with his finger to his mouth to be silent. They both crouched, hearts racing and trying desperately to hold their breath for fear of being heard.

They heard footsteps approaching fast, then pass them by and carry on along the path. Jack half stood for a better look, but Emmie pulled him down again – "Wait," she said, "he might come back."

A moment or two passed and then they heard heavy footsteps coming back towards them, slower this time. A second set of footsteps approached from the other direction, then stopped. 'Excuse me, Sir', they heard from behind the bush, 'you haven't seen a couple of oddly-dressed kids, have you?' The reply was muffled but sounded negative. Jack and Emmie froze, pressing themselves close to the ground. 'Well, if you do, please call the station', the voice continued, 'you never know who's who these days.'

At this point, both sets of footsteps started to walk away, though not before the pair overheard the last chilling words of the conversation – 'No, I'm not saying they're spies, Sir, just that you never know...'

Choosing A Disguise

Emmie listened hard to see if there were any more footsteps approaching. Everything seemed quiet, with just a background hum of traffic and the odd bird calling. It smelled fusty behind the rhododendron bush and Emmie wrinkled her nose. She moved forward in a crouched position, peering around the side of the bush, before turning to Jack and grinning. "Coast's clear," she said quietly, "good job you decided to run though."

They stood up and walked out from behind the greenery, re-joining the path as if nothing had happened. Jack pointed to a side gate, visible in the distance. "Let's head over there," he suggested shakily, "we don't want to run into that copper again!"

As they left the Gardens and turned onto the pavement once more, Emmie's thoughts returned to their predicament. "I don't think we should just stay round here," she explained, "people are more likely to notice us and wonder why we aren't at school if they keep seeing us." She paused for a moment before attempting a joke - "We don't want to be mistaken for spies – they might lock us up." Jack looked at her strangely and she realised it was a bit too real to be funny.

Just then, a red bus rumbled past them and Emmie looked at it wistfully. It was a bus where all this had started, and she felt sure that a bus would also be the key to getting home again. The problem was – how?

Jack snapped Emmie out of her contemplation. "How about looking down this way?" he asked, pointing to a road which led them away from the upcoming Tube station. They stood at the edge of the pavement, waiting for a gap in the passing mix of buses and vans, before quickly walking to the other side. As they turned into the side street which Jack had indicated, they both caught a whiff of burning in the air.

"I wonder what's on fire," Emmie pondered out loud, "I can't see any smoke."

"Me either," replied Jack, "but the smell is getting stronger."

As they rounded a bend in the road, they found the source of the smell. There was a house, or rather there had been a house – it was now largely just rubble, with smouldering wooden beams sticking out of the adjoining home. What had once been a fairly big semi-detached house now mostly just had little fragments of floor and wallpaper clinging to the wall that it used to share with the next-door house.

Jack and Emmie stared with a mixture of fascination and horror – it had been one thing to see the row of destroyed shops earlier but this was someone's home. It was even possible to make out that one of the rooms had been a child's bedroom, with animal print wallpaper and a cracked mirror still attached to the wall.

A few people walked past as they stood staring but seemed not to notice the bombed-out house. "How can they just carry on as if nothing has happened?" asked Jack. "That's someone's house..." His voice wavered a bit, and Emmie put an arm round his shoulder.

"Come on," she said, "I'm fairly sure this wasn't unusual in 1940. They're not uncaring, they're just getting on with things as best they can."

They both found it hard to draw their eyes away from the haunting spectacle of the ruined house and, as they walked further down the road, discovered that it wasn't unusual at all. Every house had brown tape in diagonal stripes across their window panes and there were three other houses with some kind of damage, although not as bad as the destroyed house.

There were a few people about – mainly women – but what was obviously a residential street was quiet overall.

At the end of the street stood a large building alongside a church – there was a small queue of people on the pavement outside. As they got closer, Jack and Emmie could smell something cooking for the second time that morning. They joined the queue and waited quietly.

Emmie nudged Jack and whispered, "Stay close to that lady in front and people will think we're together."

"Why?" whispered Jack, in a puzzled reply.

"We don't want anyone else asking why we're not at school. If we get into trouble, like with the policeman earlier, then we might not be able to get home," Emmie said, moving closer to Jack.

"How do you mean?" asked Jack, a worried expression on his face.

"Well, if someone suspects we're alone then they might try and take us into care or something like that." Jack looked horrified at the thought of this and quickly shuffled closer to the lady ahead of them.

The queue moved slowly and they eventually found themselves in the doorway of the church hall. Inside, they could see lots of benches and tables with people sitting and eating. They kept close to the woman in front of them, whilst trying not to draw her attention. As they reached the large wooden serving hatch, she suddenly turned round and looked at them. "Looks like dumplings today," she remarked, before taking the offered plate and moving along to collect some cutlery.

Emmie had been holding her breath the whole time and quickly recovered herself as Jack nudged her in the back. An older lady behind the serving hatch was holding out a plate to her and Emmie took it, smiling her thanks. They moved along the line and then made their way to a corner of the hall to sit and eat.

Emmie looked down at her plate – there were two dumplings, some thin looking gravy and a mound of green cabbage. She smiled at Jack and began to eat. The dumplings were a bit tasteless and spongy but it was warm and filled them up.

There was the rattling of a trolley behind them. "Would you like some tea?" asked a voice, which turned out to belong to another old lady, with a grey bun in her hair.

"Yes please," replied Jack, "both with milk." He added his thanks as the mugs were set down on the table. As they sipped their tea, the conversation turned to what they should do next.

"I think we should try to blend in a bit more," suggested Emmie. "Our school stuff looks a bit too new alongside most of these people. I wonder if that's what drew the policeman's attention earlier? He might have been joking about the spy thing, but we certainly look different to everyone else."

Jack looked at his own clothes – blazer and trousers – and then at Emmie who was dressed the same but with a skirt. "I noticed a box of clothes as we came in," he said, "maybe we could have a look through there and see if anything fits?"

"Good idea," Emmie agreed, "it was a bit cold in the station last night too – I could do with some kind of coat."

Once they had finished their tea, they headed over to the box of clothes near the door. There was a hand-written sign on the box which said 'Help for bombed out families'.

"Do you think it's ok to take these?" asked Jack. "Seems a bit wrong since we're not bombed out."

"Maybe…" replied Emmie, "but we've got nowhere to stay either, so it's probably ok."

There was a wide assortment of clothes in the box but eventually Jack found a black felt coat which was a bit large but would do. Emmie took a turn to rummage around and came out with a grey woollen duffel coat with a few missing toggles, but a belt which kept it together.

"How's this?" she asked.

"Yes - you look more like everyone else now, for sure," Jack replied.

They walked back out into the autumn sunshine and carried on down the street, feeling a lot less conspicuous in their new coats. Jack stopped momentarily and scuffed his shoes against a nearby wall. "What are you doing that for?" asked Emmie.

"Well, we've changed our top layers, but our shoes still look really new and shiny," Jack explained.

"Good point," agreed Emmie, following his example and roughing up the surface of her own shoes.

Later that day, after a thorough exploration of the streets to the east of the Gardens, Jack and Emmie found themselves approaching the Tube station once again.

"Should we try and sleep down there again tonight?" Jack suggested. "I don't know whether people do when there's not an air raid, but at least there were beds."

There were a few people entering the station and no one seemed to be stopping them, despite the signs by the door proclaiming that it wasn't an official shelter.

"Come on then," agreed Emmie, and they crossed the road to the station entrance. As they descended the main staircase, there was a stale smell wafting up.

Jack sniffed the air – "Guess that's what happens

when hundreds of people sleep in a cramped space," he said. "At least it's a bed though."

They walked onto the platform – the rows of bunks were quite quiet for now and Emmie noticed that at the other end to where they had slept last night was a sign for the toilets. "That's helpful," she gestured towards the sign, "I didn't notice those before."

Jack sat down on a bunk about halfway along the platform and sighed. "All that walking has tired me out." He swung his legs onto the bunk and stretched out. Emmie sat on the end and slid her school bag underneath.

"I wonder how busy it will be tonight?" She spoke quietly – even though there were only a few people around, the shape of the tunnel amplified any noise.

At that moment, a procession of people started filtering through the platform entrance – mostly women with children and older people. A lot of them were carrying bags, and Emmie noticed how tired and worn the faces were that moved past her and along the platform.

A young boy, with a side parting and glasses, stared at Emmie as he walked past, accompanied by a short woman with curly hair and an older man. Emmie stared back and wondered why he was looking at her. The family sat down further along the platform and the boy shyly walked back towards Emmie.

"Hello," he said as he approached. He was wearing a coat with frayed cardigan cuffs poking out of the sleeves and spoke with a slight accent. "My name is Jan – you say it Y.A.N. – I saw you crying in here last night – are you ok now?"

Emmie felt a knot in her stomach tighten and suddenly she was back in that awful moment of realisation yesterday.

6

The Shelter

Pulling herself together, Emmie smiled at the boy. "Hi Jan, I'm Emmie," she said, "and this is Jack."

"Hi," Jack slid his legs off the bunk and sat up.

Jan looked a bit uncertain and then moved closer to them. "Are you ok?" he repeated his question.

"Yes, thanks," Emmie answered, "I'd just had a bit of a shock yesterday, that's all. Why don't you come and sit down with us?"

Jan looked back towards Mama – she was busy with her knitting and didn't look up. She was used to him running off and playing along the platform – it was what most of the children did in the early evening to pass the time.

Jack moved up a little and Jan squeezed onto the end of the bunk. "What were you shocked about?" he asked Emmie.

"Well, it all started yesterday," Emmie began, "we were on the bus, coming home from school when there was this big flash..."

Jack nudged Emmie sharply with his elbow at this

point. She turned to him in surprise and saw him mouth 'No'. Suddenly, she realised it might not be a good idea to tell a stranger exactly what had happened – just in case. It wasn't like the last 24 hours had been exactly normal!

"Anyway," she continued, thinking quickly, "there was this flash and a huge plume of smoke from further down the road."

"A policeman told us that there had probably been a gas leak," added Jack. "We had to walk the rest of the way home and then, when we got there, we found it was a house in our street."

"Mum had been injured and was being taken off in an ambulance, and we weren't allowed back into the house as it wasn't safe," explained Emmie. The story was coming out much easier than either of them had thought.

"What about your dad?" asked Jan, "is he away?"

Emmie nodded – so many fathers were away fighting that it seemed the obvious answer.

"So, you're on your own at the moment?" Jan looked at Emmie and then Jack, "I know what that feels like."

"Jan, what are you doing?" called a voice from further down the platform. It was Mama, who had looked up from her knitting and realised Jan was almost out of sight.

"Back soon," said Jan, quickly getting up and running back down the platform.

Emmie looked at Jack – "That was close," she said. "You were right to nudge me – we should be careful what we say to people."

"First priority is to get home," agreed Jack, "we don't want to do anything to make that more difficult. I think we should focus on trying to get to the right bus stop – that old shop may give us a clue as well."

Just then, Jan came back over, bringing a halt to their conversation. "Would you like to me show you around down here?" he asked. "There's actually quite a lot to do if you know where to look."

"Sure," replied Jack. "Sounds like fun. Emmie – do you want to come too?"

"I'll stay here for a bit – I'm quite tired," she said, easing her legs onto the bunk.

Jack followed Jan back down the platform and right to the end. When they got to the white tiled wall, Jan jumped down onto the track bed and headed into the tunnel. It was brightly lit, and the rows of bunks continued as far as you could see.

"There's no track because they haven't quite finished the station yet," explained Jan. "This might be useful to you though." They had arrived at a small opening in the tunnel wall and Jack could see a kitchen set up in the space beyond. "They give out free meals each evening, normally about 7pm," Jan went on. "There's usually a big queue though, so you need to get here early."

They carried on down the tunnel and eventually it opened out again into a wide area with a brick wall at the end. The rows of bunks stopped and there was a large pile of concrete railway sleepers in the corner. "This is where the station was going to connect to the rest of the Tube," Jan told Jack. "The trains run just past that brick wall."

"What else happens in here?" asked Jack. It seemed odd that the bunks stopped at the entrance to such a large space.

"Mama said it was going to be an underground factory," Jan said, gesturing around the empty space. "They were going to make radios down here but it never happened. Sometimes we play football or hide and seek." He pointed to the corner with the pile of sleepers – "That's a great place to hide."

They looked around for a few minutes, Jack still surprised by the enormity of the space. "Come on," Jan tugged his arm, "we should get back."

Once they arrived back at the platform, Jan went to find Mama, and Jack told Emmie about their adventure in the tunnels. "The best bit is finding somewhere else to get some food," she said with a smile. "I'm quite tired now, do you think we should get some sleep?"

"Good plan," agreed Jack, clambering onto the bunk above Emmie and laying his new coat over himself as a blanket. "Night, Emmie."

"Night," murmured Emmie, sleepily.

"Jack!" came a whisper a few minutes later – it was Jan, calling from below him. Jack lifted his head and looked down. "Do you want to meet me after school tomorrow? I can show you around a bit more then. How about 4 o'clock outside the station?"

"Thanks, we'll see you then," replied Jack, before settling back onto his bunk and wondering what adventures they would find tomorrow.

The next afternoon, Jack and Emmie were waiting outside the station entrance when they saw a small figure making its way down the pavement towards them. As the figure got closer, they saw it was Jan, still wearing the same clothes from yesterday and with his cardboard gas mask case bumping against his side.

"Hi Emmie, hi Jack!" said Jan, excitedly.

"Hi Jan," they replied in unison. Jan's enthusiasm was infectious and seeing him helped dial down some of the anxiety they were both feeling.

"I've got somewhere exciting to show you," Jan

explained, pointing across the road. "Come this way."

They crossed the road together and walked in the direction that Jack and Emmie had taken the previous day.

"There's something I've been meaning to ask you," Jan turned round to face them. "Why don't you carry your gas masks? Mama won't let me leave the house without mine."

Emmie looked at Jack, "They were in our house," she answered. "We didn't take them to school on that day and then we weren't allowed back in."

"Ah, I see," Jan smiled, "we've not done any gas drills at school for ages, so I'm not really sure why I still have to carry mine either."

They walked on down the road and round the bend, before coming to the bomb-damaged house which they'd seen yesterday. It was still just as sad looking – wallpaper fragments flapping in the breeze and the smell of smouldering timber on the air.

"Here we are," said Jan, stopping and pointing to the house.

"What? Here?" said Jack, in surprise. "There's nothing here apart from a pile of rubble. There might be dead bodies in there too..."

"It's fine," replied Jan. "I heard someone talking about this house in the station the other night. There were two people who lived in it, and they were both in a shelter when the bomb hit."

"It looks like there was a child living there too," said Emmie, pointing up at the animal print wallpaper.

"Their children were evacuated to the countryside," replied Jan, "a lot of children from London were last year - at the start of the war. My school is only half full as most of them are still away."

"Ok" - Jack gestured at the house, "what's here then?"

Jan led them around the side of the house, taking care to avoid the edge of the pile of rubble. There was a large garden behind the house, with a brick outbuilding, a vegetable patch and a curious mound of earth at the bottom.

"What's that?" asked Jack, indicating the earth mound. He could now see that it had an opening at one end.

"It's the Anderson shelter," Jan answered. These arch-shaped, corrugated metal shelters had popped up in large numbers of back gardens over the past year. They were distributed for free from the local authorities and designed to keep families safe during bombing raids. "Come and have a look inside," he suggested.

"Is it safe?" asked Emmie uncertainly.

"Yes, I've been inside loads of times," replied Jan. "I've started to come and play here after school –

Mama thinks I'm playing with the other boys in my class, but I don't really get along with them."

They each ducked through the entrance to the shelter in turn. It was small inside, with two bunks along each wall, and it smelled a bit odd.

"I'm not sure I'd like to spend too many nights in here," said Emmie, shivering a little at the thought. "Come on, let's get back out into the daylight."

"The vegetable garden has lots of things in it," Jan told them as they ducked back out of the shelter. "I think the bomb damage was quite recent and all of the vegetables are ready to eat. Let's have a look."

As they walked across the garden, Emmie looked uncertain – "Isn't it stealing to take these vegetables?" she wondered out loud. "They're not ours – it feels wrong."

"The people won't be coming back any time soon," Jan said. "There are houses all around here with bomb damage and, once the owners have taken what they can, the Council or the Army will start to clear the rubble. It's not stealing – these people have chosen to leave what's in the garden."

"I suppose so," agreed Jack, "we do need to find food and we can't always rely on the soup kitchens or canteen in the station."

"I'd ask you to come home with me," said Jan, "but Mama doesn't have the room, I'm afraid."

"It's ok," replied Jack, "hopefully it'll only be for a few days and then Mum will be out of hospital. How about we meet you here again tomorrow afternoon, Jan?"

"Good idea," Jan said, with a grin. He waved as he ran back through the garden, leaving Jack and Emmie to decide where to spend the night.

"I think we'll have to head to the station soon," suggested Emmie. "I'd like to get a decent spot." Jack looked downcast at the thought of another night in the station. "What's up?" asked Emmie gently.

"It's getting home – I just don't know how we're going to do it..."

"What happened to all that confidence earlier?" she joked. "You were all for finding another route to the right bus stop."

"I know – I still think that's what we should try next," he answered in a quiet voice. "There's always something though – first the unexploded bomb, then the conductor on the bus, then that policeman..." His voice trailed off and Emmie gave his arm a supportive squeeze. "I'm still struggling to believe that it's possible to time travel and, if it is, it feels like someone has stitched the hole in time back up and trapped us here."

Spies

As they climbed the steps from the station, Emmie turned to Jack – "Are you ok?" she asked. "You seem very quiet this morning."

"I'm still thinking about last night," said Jack, quietly. His head was down and he didn't make eye contact. "It feels like we're stuck here, and I'm scared we'll never get back."

Emmie nodded slowly, guiding them to the right as they exited the station. "I know what you mean," she replied, "this has blown my mind too, and I'm as unsure as you are about what to do next." A thin smile then began to spread across her face – "Except, right now, it's time to find some food!"

Jack nodded – he didn't feel like returning the smile, but he was definitely hungry. They'd had some bread from the kitchen in the shelter the night before - it hadn't really filled them up, but it stopped them being hungry when they were trying to sleep.

They walked down the side of the Gardens, heading for the soup kitchen that they'd found in the church hall previously. It was a mild morning, with a few leaves starting to fall from the trees along the pavement, and there seemed to be more people about than usual. As they crossed the road, Jack looked up and saw an olive-green truck with soldiers sitting in the back go slowly past. He stared at them – most didn't look much older than he and Emmie, yet they were ready to fight for their country. Letting out an involuntary shiver, he pulled his coat a little tighter around him.

Emmie noticed the soldiers too – "I guess they're training," she said, "they don't really look old enough to fight yet."

"I think you're right about the training," replied Jack. "I think this is after the Dunkirk evacuation, so most of the soldiers we have are back in Britain now."

"Yes, I remember from school that the evacuation was in the early summer of 1940," Emmie agreed.

They neared the soup kitchen and saw there was a larger queue than before. As they joined the back of it, Emmie noticed that Jack was still looking glum. "Cheer up," she said, "everything will feel a lot better when we've had some breakfast."

They shuffled forward in the queue over the next 10 minutes, slowly getting closer to the door. There was a pleasant smell coming from the hall, but it was difficult to tell exactly what it was. As they reached the door and filed inside, they could see that most of the tables were full, which was contributing to the slow speed of the queue. Finally, they reached the serving hatch and were grateful to receive a couple of slices of bread, a bowl of porridge and a mug of tea. Piling these onto wooden trays, Emmie turned to look for space to sit down. The hall was still full so they asked an old couple if they might join them at their table.

As they sat down, Emmie leaned over to Jack and said she was just going to find the toilet. Jack began to eat his porridge hungrily, watched by the old couple.

"Are you alright, son?" the elderly man asked after a while. "Don't you get fed at home?" His wife looked at Jack too, with a concerned expression on her face.

Suddenly, Jack felt overwhelmed with their situation, put his head in his hands and started to sob. Big tears fell from his face onto the wooden tabletop and his shoulders shook. He lifted his bag onto the table and scrabbled around in it for something to wipe his face. In his anxious state, Jack managed to upend the bag onto the table, and everything inside fell out.

"Here, take this" – the woman handed him a handkerchief, whilst her husband stared curiously at the contents of Jack's bag. He pointed at a calculator – "What's that?" he asked.

"Oh, nothing," Jack said absently, putting it back

into the bag. "Thank you," he mumbled to the woman through his tears, and dabbed at his face.

"So, why are you here?" she carried on, gently. "Shouldn't you be at school, or with your mum?"

At the mention of his mum, Jack's face crumpled even further. "We're lost…" he blurted out, "we're lost, and we can't work out how to get home…" He was shocked at himself, even through his tears – he hadn't meant to tell anyone the truth but simply couldn't carry the weight of it any more.

"How do you mean? Where do you live?"

"We were on the bus and then there was this flash, you see," Jack carried on, his voice still shaky.

The couple were looking increasingly concerned as Emmie returned to the table. Noticing the tension, she put an arm around Jack's shoulder – "Ok now?" she asked.

"He's been telling us that you're lost," the old man explained. "Can we help at all?" He kept looking at Jack's bag as he said this.

Emmie quickly recounted their previous story – telling the couple that they had been bombed out and their mother was in hospital.

"Well, if you're sure we can't help…" replied the old man, finishing his tea. "I hope your mother is better soon." He stood and began to clear their plates onto a tray.

"Thank you," said Emmie, smiling brightly at them. "Bye," she added as they walked away to return their trays.

"What was that all about, and what happened to your bag?" she asked, turning to Jack. "We've got to be really careful about what we say to people."

"Sorry," he sniffed, "I just felt so alone... I tried to wipe my face and spilled everything out of my bag."

"Well, I'm here so it's going to be ok." Emmie gave his arm a squeeze - "Let's finish our breakfast before anything else happens."

They cleared their plates gratefully, Jack feeling a lot better now he'd had some food. They piled the empty crockery back onto a tray and Jack carried it over to the service hatch. Pulling their coats on, they turned to leave. The room was still very full and there was a moderate level of chatter coming from most of the tables. As they headed across the room to the door, a policeman walked in through it, tall in his dark uniform and helmet. Behind him, Emmie could see the old couple from their table. Instinctively, she tugged Jack's arm, pulling him close to the thick curtains which hung around the room. They froze, watching the policeman start to scan the room and the old couple point towards the corner where they had been sitting.

"Behind here," whispered Emmie, parting the

curtains. They slipped through them, just in time to hear the background noise decrease as the tables of people began to notice the presence of the policeman. Emmie looked around behind the curtain – there was just a wall running along most of this side of the room but further along there was a window.

"Do you think we can slip along to that window?" asked Jack, guessing what she was thinking.

"Let's give it a go," Emmie answered quietly, shuffling sideways whilst trying not to move the curtain in front of her. Jack followed, conscious that his feet were probably sticking out beneath the curtain.

They reached the window without further event, and Emmie felt behind her, trying to open the catch. It was stiff and she was aware that forcing it would probably make a noise. She could hear the policeman a few tables away asking people if they had seen a boy and girl matching their description. She wondered why the old couple had found a policeman – obviously something that Jack had said concerned them – hopefully they were just trying to help but Emmie didn't think it worth staying around to find out.

Eventually, after a lot of wiggling, she managed to free the window catch. "Are you ready to climb through?" she asked Jack. "Once this opens, the curtain will blow about, and we'll have to move really fast."

"Yes, I'm ready," Jack whispered back, slipping his school bag off his shoulder.

Emmie pushed the window open with a creaking noise. She held her breath for a second, then decided it was now or never, turned and half climbed, half forward rolled through the window.

"STOP!" came a shout from the other side of the curtain and Jack scrambled through the window after Emmie. A hand pulled the curtain sharply open and Jack felt a tug on his ankle. He shook his leg furiously and felt the grip loosen, only to be reapplied to the bag in his left hand, still dangling down inside the window. As he half fell to the ground, still holding onto the bag strap, he looked up to see the angry face of the policeman leaning through, his hand firmly on the other strap. In that split second, Jack decided the bag was too important to let go and tugged it hard. One of the pockets tore and some of the contents fell out for the second time that morning. As he jerked free and ran after Emmie, he realised that the pocket had a lot of his modern-day schoolwork in. That would look really odd to someone in 1940 when they went through it.

As he caught up with Emmie, they raced down the road and along a path behind a small warehouse. He pulled her down behind a low wall and, as they lay there panting, wondering if anyone was giving chase, she noticed the torn pocket on his bag.

"Oh no, Jack," she said, despairingly, "when someone finds your things, they're going to know something's up and that we're not just regular 1940's kids. We're going to have to be so careful from now on..." She looked up at him – "What was the old man looking at? Whatever it was certainly seemed to spook him."

"It was my calculator," said Jack sadly. He was quiet for a moment, thinking. "Gosh," he said, "they might actually have thought we were spies... It would certainly explain why they fetched a policeman."

8

What's For Breakfast?

Stan walked slowly along the pavement, keeping his head down and his dark overcoat drawn around himself. The autumn morning had yet to warm up and the London streets were quiet. There hadn't been any planes over last night and the day felt calmer already as a result. His eyes darted left and right, taking in his surroundings. He passed a fish and chip shop and stopped briefly, his hunger drawing him to the smells coming from inside. As he turned left at the corner of the street, he noticed a narrow alley way, running back towards the shop. Quickly, he glanced around him and then, satisfied that there was no-one about, ducked into the alley.

It was dirty and a bit overgrown, running between buildings of various sizes and clearly only used as a route to take bins out. As he neared the back of the fish and chip shop, he paused and listened. Silence. He carried on slowly, still unsure exactly what he might find at the end.

The alley opened out into a flagstone covered yard behind the shop. There was a grimy window and a doorway with a bead curtain moving gently in the breeze. Stan could hear noises coming from inside – the bubble of the fryer and the chopping of potatoes. There was a row of bins along the side of the shop and it was these that Stan was most interested in.

He waited for a few moments more, watching and listening, before slowly creeping over to the nearest bin and lifting the lid. It was empty. He tried the next one and found that it was full of potato sacks, with a thin layer of peelings on the top. He was tempted to grab a handful of the peelings to dull his hunger but decided to try the last bin first. As he tried to lift the lid, it caught on a rough part of the wall behind and made a loud clang. Stan hurriedly put it down again.

"Oi, what's going on out there?!" a loud voice shouted from the doorway. Stan didn't stop to look as he turned to run back down the alley. "Come here, you little thief!" the voice shouted, and Stan was aware of a figure coming from his left as he reached the narrow entrance. He ran as fast as he could, emerging back onto the street and nearly colliding with several people on the pavement, before dodging behind a thick hedge and pressing himself into it. He panted heavily and squeezed himself even further into the hedge. As he fought to get his breathing under control, he tried to listen for anyone chasing him. The blood was pounding in his ears but, as it subsided, he could tell that there were only regular footsteps coming from the other side of the hedge – people walking past normally, rather than giving chase.

Stan waited a few long minutes to be sure that no-one was pursuing him and then slowly eased himself out from the hedge. He patted his coat down to remove the bits of leaf and then walked back around the hedge to continue in the same direction.

He was really hungry – there had been nothing to eat in the house when he had got up and Mrs Smith was still asleep. She often did this – stayed up into the small hours and then didn't surface until mid-morning. Stan's best option was to try and find something to eat for himself.

He was a tall boy, with a long, serious face and, unfortunately, over the past year had found very little to like about his new life in London. He had arrived after a long sea and rail journey, and initially had no foster family to go to. He had stayed in a transit camp on the Suffolk coast for 2 weeks until Mrs Smith had been found to take him in. It hadn't been too unusual an experience for a boy who had spent most of his life in a Jewish orphanage in Poland. He was used to care from adults but not really much affection, so being at the end of queue for a family didn't faze him much. The tiny room he lived in at Mrs Smith's, however, wasn't a patch on the large orphanage dormitory and he found the nights very long and lonely.

As he walked down the street, he reflected on how

similar parts of London were to the city of Poznan where he had grown up. The orphanage had been on the edge of the city and it was a happy place, with about 100 children living there. When it looked like war in Europe was certain, the orphanage had arranged to send its children abroad for their safety, and that was how Stan had found himself on a steam ship, crossing first the Baltic and then the North Sea, en-route to England. He had travelled as part of a group with about 20 others, looked after by one of the teachers from their school.

A little further on, Stan saw a boarded-up bakery. It looked like the boarding up had happened recently, though there was no visible damage to the outside. Stan looked around for a passage leading to the rear of the shop but there was nothing obvious. It was too dangerous to try and get in from the front as there were quite a few people about. He was really hungry but not yet desperate enough to risk getting into any real trouble. There was always a worry at the back of his mind that he'd be sent away – Mrs Smith barely looked after him, but at least he had a bed to sleep in and a roof over his head.

A passing van jolted Stan out of his thoughts – he looked up and saw that it was a mobile soup kitchen. He had seen it before, parked outside the Tube station sometimes in a morning. As he watched, the van slowed and entered a nearby square, before stopping at the kerbside. He generally avoided places where lots of other people congregated, as he didn't want to be asked why he wasn't at school, but maybe this time it would be alright. He was hungry enough to risk taking the chance.

Stan walked closer to the van and sat down on a bench just across the road, where he could keep a discreet lookout. He hunched down into his coat and waited. Soon, there was the smell of soup being warmed up and a small queue started to form in front of the van. Once people began to be served, Stan stood up and crossed the road to join the queue. He tried to avoid eye contact with the people around him, but he needn't have worried – at nearly 6 feet tall, he would easily pass for school leaving age.

As he reached the front of the queue, Stan put his hand up to take the mug of hot soup on offer and helped himself to a thick slice of the brown bread. He hungrily bit into it as he moved away and used the mug to warm his hands. He always felt slightly cold, even on a pleasant day like today, so the soup was very welcome. Once he had finished, he smiled his thanks as he returned the mug.

Now, the question was what to do for the rest of the day. He tended to spend a lot of time walking the streets, exploring bombed-out buildings and keeping himself to himself. Stan didn't naturally avoid company but not all of his experiences in England had been positive. When he first arrived in London and started school, he was teased a lot because of his accent, and some of the children had made anti-Jewish comments. The teacher had dealt with this very firmly, but Stan was still cautious around new people as a result.

He decided to go and explore a nearby factory which had been destroyed by bombs a few weeks previously. There was a big metal fence around the edge of the site, but Stan had discovered a gap along the side which was possible to slip through. The factory appeared to have made paint and in some of the less damaged parts it was possible to see the large mixing vats and machinery used to create the paint.

As Stan wriggled though the gap in the fence, trying not to snag his coat on the wire, he wondered if there would be another air raid that night. He hated being shut in the shelter when there was a raid going on – it was obviously much safer but the brick structures which had appeared in their street the previous spring were crowded and damp. There were bunks bolted three high against the wall and often there were at least two people to each bed. The shelters had very basic facilities and he always worried he might need to use the toilet – this was no more than a bucket in the corner, with an old sheet pegged around it. Sometimes Mrs Smith would take him to the nearest Tube station but typically they went to the street shelter as it was almost right outside the house.

Once inside the paint factory, Stan wandered around, fascinated at what he could see. He liked to imagine that he worked in such a place and all the levers and handles did amazing things when he operated them. One day, when the war was over, he thought that he would like a job in a factory.

All too soon, Stan noticed the daylight fading and realised that he ought to start making his way back home to Mrs Smith. The blackout was strictly enforced after dark and it was quite difficult to find your way about if you were in unfamiliar streets. Stan knew the area fairly well but it was still better not to be out unnecessarily. He slipped back out through the gap in the fence and began to trudge home.

9

The Stranger

It was mid-morning – Jack and Emmie had spent another night in the Tube station and were finding it hard to sleep properly in such a crowded environment. It was stuffy, noisy and a bit smelly and, although they felt safe, it wasn't a pleasant experience. Emmie had needed to queue for the toilet for half an hour during the night and commented to Jack on her return how much she was missing being able to watch TV. Before they settled down for the night, Jack had ventured back to the bricked off end of the tunnel that Jan had showed him previously, but there hadn't been anyone playing there.

"We need a new plan to get home," Emmie announced, as they walked along the pavement together. It was a cool morning, with some early autumn sun and a bit of a breeze.

"What do you suggest?" asked Jack. "We tried the bus idea and it didn't work."

"Well, kind of," replied Emmie, "we didn't really get a chance to see if it worked or not – the road was blocked and we were kicked off too soon anyway."

"We really need to get some old money from somewhere. I wonder if we can get a job or something like that?" Jack kicked a stone along in front of him as he spoke.

"Hmm, but what kind of job?" mused Emmie. "I can't see anyone wanting to give a couple of school kids a job."

Jack looked up – they were approaching the bridge near the bus stop where their adventure had started. "How about we look for that shop again?" he suggested, "you know, the one with the gas mask in the window. Maybe that will help somehow?"

Emmie looked at him – "Good idea," she replied. "I don't know how it was connected but I definitely hadn't seen that shop before."

They crossed the road and saw that their way was still blocked with rubble. "Great…" said Jack sarcastically.

Emmie pointed further along the road, in the direction the bus had taken them the other day – "Look," she said, "that road runs parallel to where we want to be." She led them to it and they found themselves walking along a largely residential street, with side roads which led down to the blocked route. Frustratingly, each side road also had a barrier at the end, preventing easy entry to where they wanted to be.

They looked down the first side road - there was a butcher and a pawnbroker close to a bus stop sign, but no blue shop. "I'm sure it was just before the bus stop," Jack said.

"Let's walk along the road a bit further," suggested Emmie, "maybe it wasn't as close to the bus stop as you remember?"

They carried along the road for another few minutes, peering down each side road in turn, but there was no blue shop to be seen. A couple of red buses passed by, and Jack nearly put his hand out to stop them - each one had a conductor standing on the back step though, so he was glad that he hadn't.

"I can't understand how the shop could vanish," Emmie said, as they slowed outside a greengrocer. There were lots of vegetables stacked up in the window and they both felt hungry at the sight of them.

"I think we need to sit and have a proper discussion if we're going to solve this problem today. Let's find something to eat whilst we talk." Jack was looking hungrily in the greengrocer's window. "Shall we head back to that soup kitchen where we got the coats?"

"We should probably avoid going to the same places too often." Emmie hesitated before carrying on – she was hungry too but had been spooked by their two brushes with policemen. "Shall we see if the WVS van is at the station today?"

They walked back down the road, noticing that a large queue had formed at the butchers. Emmie saw that a chalkboard outside had 'Sausages and beef in today' written on it. The people in the queue were chattering excitedly, and Emmie realised that these foods they might normally take for granted were in really short supply in 1940.

As they passed the large pile of rubble again, with its unexploded bomb sign, and reached the junction with the Tube station on, Jack craned his neck to see if the WVS van was parked outside. "I can't see it," he said disappointedly. They crossed the road and walked up to the station entrance to make sure. There was definitely no van and the whole pavement area outside the station was very quiet.

"I wonder if the van is only here first thing and when there has been an air raid?" wondered Emmie. "I guess they have a lot of people all over London to help out."

"Doesn't help us," replied Jack sulkily. "I'm hungry." He sat down on the wall outside the Gardens. It was a low wall, and you could see where some railings had been cut down recently to provide metal to support the war effort.

"Come on, Jack," Emmie sat down next to him. "It's getting to me too, but we just need to look after ourselves until we can work out how to get to the right bus stop. Hopefully, they'll clear that rubble in a day or two and unblock the road." She looked up – "How about we go back to that ruined house Jan showed us and dig up a few vegetables?"

"I suppose so…" Jack agreed. "Jan said he'd meet us there again later, so we can always explore in the meantime."

As they approached the bombed-out house, Jack felt a little better. "Thanks Emmie," he said, "I just don't know how we're going to get back and it's making me feel down."

"I know," Emmie put an arm around his shoulder, "me too. We'll figure it out though."

Once in the garden, they headed for the vegetable plot. "Are you sure this is ok?" asked Jack. "I know Jan said yesterday that people take everything they want from a damaged house and then leave it but even so…"

"I know what you mean," agreed Emmie, "but I think it's fine in the circumstances. We'll only take what we actually need."

"Ok…" Jack conceded and pulled up a couple of carrots. They were covered in dark, heavy soil but looked really thick and juicy. "Just need to find somewhere to wash them now," he said. Over by the brick outbuilding was a tap and Jack headed towards it.

"Be careful of any broken glass," warned Emmie. Although the houses in the street had brown tape on their windows to stop glass flying in an explosion, no-one had thought to do so with the outbuilding. The small window adjacent to the door had jagged remnants of glass in it and Emmie guessed there would be glass all over the ground as well.

"Got it," Jack shouted over his shoulder. Emmie still heard the crunching of glass under his feet, so it didn't seem that Jack had listened that well after all.

As he returned with the clean carrots, Jack handed one to Emmie and then took a bite out of his. "Mmm," he said, "I don't think I've ever had a carrot that fresh before."

Emmie ate hers hungrily too − "Me either," she responded, "they're so crunchy."

Feeling slightly less hungry now, they decided to have a look around the rest of the garden to see what else there might be. As they rounded the corner of the outbuilding, Jack noticed an apple tree growing close to the wall. There were a few windfalls already on the grass and a heavy crop of red apples still on the tree.

"Bingo," he said, "I love an apple." He reached up into the tree and plucked a couple from a convenient branch. "Here you go" - he offered one to Emmie.

"Shall we go for a wander until Jan gets here? People might see us hanging around in the garden otherwise," Emmie suggested. She was a little concerned that locals would notice them, despite it being very quiet in the street outside. "We're less likely to get awkward questions if we don't stay in the same place too long."

"Yes – good idea," Jack agreed. "We should go the other way at the end of the road and see what's up there."

They spent the next hour walking around residential streets which were largely quite deserted. "It's a bit of a ghost town, isn't it?" said Emmie.

"I guess people are out at work and school," replied Jack. "A lot of the men will be away at war too."

"Yes, I remember that from school," Emmie explained, "women moved into a lot of the jobs previously done by men, as they weren't around." She thought for a moment – "It's very different to today, isn't it? Men and women do the same jobs now but in 1940 it was probably a novelty."

Just before 4, Jack checked his watch and they changed direction back to the house to meet Jan. As they approached, they could see him sitting on the front wall, swinging his legs. "Hello," he called, as they approached. "What have you been up to?"

Emmie gave him a quick account of their day, leaving out the details about looking for the blue shop.

Jan was fast becoming their friend, but it still felt risky revealing to him exactly what had happened - besides, they still weren't quite sure themselves.

"How about we have a look in that shelter again?" suggested Jack. It might be nicer to stay in there than down in the Tube station.

Emmie looked uncertain – "It was quite small and didn't smell any better," she replied, but she followed Jan and Jack around the side of the ruined house anyway.

Jack was pointing out where they had pulled the carrots up when there was suddenly some movement from the Anderson shelter at the end of the garden. A tall, dark figure emerged from the doorway, paused to look in their direction, and then ran quickly to the wall along the rear of the garden and scrambled up onto it.

Jack shrank back towards the rubble from the house and pulled Emmie and Jan down with him. "Who was that?" he whispered.

"Did he frighten you?" asked Jan. "You look like you've seen a ghost."

"I don't know, I guess I just thought this was our place," replied Jack, quietly. "Anyway," he continued, "how do we know he wasn't up to no good..."

"There's one way to find out," said Emmie, getting up and walking over to the shelter. She bent her head through the doorway, then disappeared inside.

"What's there?" called Jack gingerly.

"Come on, let's go and see," Jan ran over to the shelter in excitement, just in time to see Emmie emerge clutching a magazine.

"Look at this," she said, her face pale. "It was open on a page about building a radio."

Jan and Jack looked at her — she handed the magazine to Jan, who opened it eagerly, and then stepped closer to Jack. "A radio, Jack," she whispered, "who hangs around in abandoned places and builds a radio...?"

10

Vegetables

"This magazine is really interesting," Jan said, flicking through the pages. "I wonder if you really can build a radio yourself?"

"Are you sure there's nothing else inside?" asked Jack. He cautiously approached the earth mound at the end of the garden and peered through the doorway. It was gloomy and the interior looked as he had remembered it. "I'll check," he volunteered, not feeling quite as brave as he sounded.

"Can you see anything else? I checked pretty well," Emmie's voice came through the doorway behind him.

"No, it's definitely empty," replied Jack. Emmie and Jan stepped in too, each taking a seat on one of the bunks. They all looked around the small space, wondering why the shadowy figure had been in there.

"You're right," Emmie said eventually, "there's nothing here."

"I wonder what he was up to?" offered Jan. "He looked too big to be playing. I'll have a look around the garden and see if I can spot anything else." Emmie picked up the magazine and handed it to Jack to slot into his rucksack.

"He might be a spy..." whispered Jack, once Jan was outside. His mind was in overdrive now, running through endless possibilities. "Maybe we should go to the police?"

"You do remember what happened last time we saw a policeman, don't you?" Emmie replied. "We drew far too much attention to ourselves, even before you lost the contents of your school bag." Jack looked down at the floor. "At least you didn't drop your calculator after that old man was so curious about it," she continued, "but if we're not careful, it's us who will be labelled spies!"

Jack looked up – "I know, I'm sorry – I didn't mean to say so much to those people in the soup kitchen..." His voice tailed off and Emmie gave him a quick smile.

"Don't worry about it – I was just trying to be realistic about what we should do," Emmie said gently. "There is one thing which keeps coming back to me though – if there is a spy, and he's successful in his mission, the war might turn out differently. If the Germans win, it might change everything – in the future I mean..."

Jack stared at Emmie in horror – "You mean, even if we get home, it might not be the same? We have to look for that person and stop him!"

Jan reappeared at this point, having scoured the garden for clues. "I couldn't find anything out there either," he explained.

"I don't think we should go back to the Tube station tonight." Jack looked up and turned to Emmie. "I think we should sleep in here instead." The thought of mixing with other people felt really unappealing to Jack after the events of the day so far.

"I guess we could..." replied Emmie, slowly. The shelter smelled a bit unpleasant, but not any worse than the station, and at least they wouldn't have to try and avoid people.

"I think it's a good idea," Jan chimed in. "You can make it comfortable whilst you wait for your mother to come out of hospital."

Emmie looked at Jack – they had both forgotten that part of the story!

A pang of guilt pricked at Emmie for how they were having to lie to their new friend. "Yes, that's right," she said hurriedly, "we're going to visit her this evening to see how she is."

"Let's see what we can find to make the shelter more comfortable for tonight," suggested Jack. "Shall we take a look in that outbuilding?"

They filed back out of the shelter and across the grass to the rear of the house. The brick outbuilding was set apart from the house by a small, paved area and it had a wooden door with a rusting latch on. Jack reached for the latch to open the door.

'Crrrreak', the hinges squealed, as the door swung open. There was some light filtering in through the broken window on the side wall and they could see rows of shelves facing a pile of coal in the opposite corner. They all squeezed in through the door and looked around.

"Candles!" said Jack excitedly. He had spotted a few white candles lying on one of the shelves, along with a glass jar which they could stand them in. "We need some matches too," he explained, looking further along the shelf.

"Here you go," cried Jan. He passed a small box to Jack, who shook it to check there were some matches inside.

"There's not a lot else of use in here," remarked Emmie. "I think we'll have to sleep in our coats tonight."

Leaving the outbuilding, they said goodbye to Jan, who was heading home for his tea. Before he left, he pressed a small parcel into Emmie's hand. "Some bread," he said, "it's not much, but it will help."

"Thanks Jan," Emmie said, giving the small boy a hug.

"Yeah, thanks," agreed Jack, smiling at him and waving as Jan walked back through the garden.

Jack and Emmie went back to the shelter, pausing to pull up a few more carrots to accompany their bread from Jan. As they ducked inside, Emmie noticed a dark curtain pinned behind the doorway.

"This must be to help with the blackout," she observed, "it'll keep the wind out a bit too." She pulled the curtain across and lit one of the candles they had found, placing it in the jar for safety.

As they settled down on the bunks to eat their food, Jack thought back over the day. It was still hurting his brain thinking about how they'd got here in the first place and their run in with the old couple and the policeman had complicated things further.

"Do you think it's safe for us to be walking about?" he asked Emmie. "I don't want us to get into trouble and not be able to get home again."

"Yes, I think so," Emmie replied. "We just need to avoid drawing attention to ourselves and probably not go to the same places too often."

"I guess so," Jack agreed, "we should get some sleep too – hopefully quieter than in the station."

"Night then," said Emmie, pulling her coat closer round her and stretching out on the bunk.

The next morning Jack woke early. There was a grey light filtering around the blackout curtain, which was flapping gently in the breeze. He looked around, wondering for a moment where he was, and then lay back on his bunk, staring at the corrugated metal roof. He had counted almost all of the bolts that he could see, when he heard stirring from the other top bunk.

"Are you awake, Jack?" murmured Emmie sleepily. She rubbed her eyes and sat up, stretching.

"Yep," answered Jack. "I've been awake for a while – didn't want to disturb you though."

Emmie smiled – "Chilly, isn't it? I wonder if we'd have been warmer in the Tube station…"

"We'll have to see what we can do to keep warmer in here, I think," replied Jack. "I felt a lot more comfortable knowing we weren't going to run into anyone else." He swung his legs over the side of the bunk and jumped down to the floor. "I've had an idea about how we can get some more interesting food too. Come on."

Emmie followed him out into the garden in the direction of the vegetable patch. "What's your idea?" she asked.

"I think we should dig up a couple of boxes of vegetables and take them to the market to sell them. It's Thursday, which means market day, even in 1940."

"How will we do that? We haven't got a stall,"

Emmie sounded surprised.

"We should just offer to sell them to one of the vegetable stallholders. It's got to be worth a try," Jack said optimistically.

"Ok, but there's a big risk of drawing attention to ourselves," warned Emmie. "If we're going to do it, we need to keep to the side streets and avoid walking through the busy parts of the market. We should try and go early too – before it gets busy."

With that, they started pulling up carrots, leeks and cabbages. Jack went into the outbuilding and came back with two small wooden crates which they piled the fresh vegetables into. "Let's go," he smiled.

They walked along the road with their boxes of vegetables, attracting a few strange looks from the early morning passers-by. No-one said anything though, which gave them more confidence in their plan. They passed the Tube station on the opposite side of the road, only crossing when they were well clear of it – just in case. They bypassed the road with the unexploded bomb and set off down the street from yesterday, looking down each side road in turn to choose the best spot to emerge into the market.

As they saw the market stalls appear in the distance, Jack paused. "I think we should scan the stalls before we approach anyone and then go for the smallest stall," he suggested. "They're probably the most likely to buy our vegetables and there will be less people around too."

He looked at the visible stalls, most having colourful canopies above them. The first stall was a fruit and vegetable stall, but it was quite big, then came a bric-a-brac stall and a man with some chickens. Down the next side road, slightly set back, was a small vegetable stall. Best of all was the realisation that the barrier at the end of the road had gone.

"That's the one," said Jack, pointing at the smaller stall. "Let's slip down the next street and we'll come out along the side of it."

They walked a bit further, as Jack had suggested, and came at the stall from the side. Jack walked confidently up to the man standing behind the display table. "Would you like to buy some more vegetables?" he said, holding up his box.

The man looked at him for a moment – "No sonny, I'm trying to sell these ones!" he replied. Jack looked crestfallen and his shoulders drooped.

Emmie stepped up to the stall, alongside Jack. "Please," she pleaded, "we're just trying to earn some money for some food."

At the mention of the word 'earn', the man's expression changed and became softer. "Fair enough," he replied, "I admire anyone who is trying to make their situation better." He put his hands out for the boxes and rifled through their contents. "Ok, how about this – I'll give you 2 shillings and you promise to buy yourself something hot to eat?"

Jack grinned at Emmie. "Deal," she said "and thank you." She put the coins in her pocket and together they turned and walked back down the street in search of some breakfast.

Kindertransport

"Have you got your bag, Jan?" asked his mother. They were waiting in the hall of their apartment block in Danzig for Jan's father to bring the car round to the door. It was mid-summer in 1939 and the day was already hot. His mother fanned her face with a magazine - she was a tall woman, with dark hair and usually had a smile on her face. Today, however, she looked both worried and serious.

Jan tapped his bag – "Yes, Mother, it's right here," he answered. He had packed as much as he'd been able into the small suitcase that his mother had chosen the day before. They had been issued with strict instructions about the size of bag permitted, and Jan's mother was keen that he followed the rules.

His mother stood up as a car rounded the corner and slowed in front of the door. Jan saw his father behind the wheel and stood too, picking up the case in his left hand. His father got out and opened the boot for Jan to put the case inside. It was slightly unnecessary as the case was so small, but his father always liked to do things right.

Jan climbed in through the rear door, held open by his father, and his mother followed. She normally sat in the front but today was going to sit alongside Jan. She took his hand in hers as the car moved off – "Promise you'll write as soon as you can?"

"Of course I will," replied Jan, "once I get to my host family, I'll write to tell you about the journey." He was feeling both excited and apprehensive about the trip. His parents had explained that it would only be for a few months and they would follow on as soon as they could.

"I do hope they're nice," said his mother, in a concerned voice.

"Jan will be fine," came the voice of his father from the front seat. He had studied in England when he was younger and was very fond of the country and the people in it. The imminent threat of war in Europe had caused Jan's parents to arrange for him to travel to England. They had seen how academics like his father had been treated in other countries occupied by the Germans and didn't want to put their only son at risk. Although deeply worried for the future, Jan's father was proud that England was to be Jan's destination.

As they arrived at the station, Jan's mother gripped his hand a little harder. He squeezed it back – he could tell that his parents were worried, but he was quite looking forward to going on a big adventure.

"We're here," announced his father somewhat unnecessarily, and opened the door for them. Jan collected his case from the boot and followed his parents into the station. A few moments later, they had located the committee organiser and Jan's name had been crossed off multiple lists.

His mother bent down to give Jan a hug – "Be good and stay safe," she said, squeezing him tightly. He squeezed her back and then took the hand his father offered.

"Good luck, son" – his father's voice faltered a little and, on impulse, he bent down to give Jan a hug too.

"Bye," managed Jan, as he was marshalled away by the committee lady, along with a group of other children. He turned to wave and saw his parents hugging each other. They waved at him and then his group rounded the corner and were out of sight.

Once on the train, Jan settled into a compartment - sitting in the corner by the window which he'd opened for some ventilation. He loved to look out and see the countryside rushing past – that was the best bit of any adventure. Shortly afterwards, there was a whistle and the train slowly puffed out of the station. There were 3 other children in Jan's compartment – two girls and a boy. The boy was much younger than Jan and the girls talked amongst themselves, so Jan had plenty of time to stare out of the window. There was a lot of farmland rushing past initially, punctuated by areas of forest.

After a few hours they were at the German border, where the train halted for what seemed like an age whilst border guards came along the carriages and inspected each person's paperwork. The committee organiser was in the next compartment to Jan, and he heard a lengthy conversation between her and the border guards. There were a lot of raised voices as names were checked and cross-checked against documents, with Jan breathing a heavy sigh of relief when the guards appeared to depart.

Some moments later, a different border guard appeared from the opposite direction and entered their compartment. "Papers!" he commanded in German. Jan knew some German from school and explained that the lady in charge was in the next compartment. The guard went to check and thankfully didn't come back.

The train eventually started to move again and headed through eastern Germany, towards the capital, Berlin. Jan's mother had packed him a sandwich and an apple and he ate these hungrily as the afternoon progressed. The girls sat opposite him spent the time either chatting or crying gently, whilst the young boy was mostly asleep.

As the light began to fade, Jan got up to stretch his

legs. He walked outside his compartment and along the carriage, looking into the other compartments as he passed. There were a lot of children his own age on this part of the train – more than had been at the station in Danzig. He supposed some of them had come from further inside Poland and already been on the train when he boarded it. As he walked back to his seat, he thought about the possibility of war. Like most children of his age, he was very aware of the Great War which had only been twenty years before – most adults didn't really talk about it in detail, but there was still a sense of its horror. He couldn't imagine that coming to his sheltered life.

He peered out through the carriage window – they were coming into a large, grey city, passing suburbs of low-rise housing and parks, with these eventually giving way to larger buildings. As they pulled into a station, he saw a large sign announcing that they were in Berlin. There were many platforms under a large, glazed metal arch roof, and their train stopped at what felt like the back of the station. As Jan looked around, he noticed there were red, white and black flags hanging from every conceivable surface, each bearing the German swastika logo. He recoiled in horror - that flag had been in many unpleasant newsreels over the past few years, which he'd seen when visiting the cinema with his parents.

Jan quickly walked back to his compartment and sat

down in the corner – this time looking in, rather than out. The quicker they left Berlin the better, as far as he was concerned. Unfortunately for Jan, this wasn't to be the case – the committee lady walked around and told them that the train was being delayed until there was space in the schedule for it to run further west. Jan shrank down into his seat, hoping that the delay wouldn't be too long. After a few minutes, he heard the barking of dogs and a crunch of footsteps on gravel outside the train. He risked a glance out of the window and saw two uniformed guards, along with a pair of fierce-looking Alsatians, walking alongside the train. They passed by several times, glaring at anyone who dared to look at them from the train window.

"Ignore them," said the committee lady, who had appeared at the compartment door to check on the children. "They're just trying to intimidate us. Hopefully we'll be going again soon."

There was a sudden jerk and Jan woke with a start. He must have fallen asleep, as it was pitch dark outside now and the train had started to move. The station was almost empty, save for a small group of soldiers who had gathered near the coffee bar, apparently waiting for a late-night train. As Jan watched, the soldiers slowly disappeared out of sight as the station fell behind them. The train gathered speed, moving out of the city centre and into the suburbs once again.

In the distance, Jan saw a large stadium, distinctive with twin columns holding up the 5 Olympic rings between them. He remembered seeing the Berlin Olympics in newsreels a few years previously and being hugely impressed by the scale of the stadium. It was large, even when viewed from a kilometre away on the train.

Jan dozed on and off for the rest of the night – the train passing through Hamburg and Bremen early the next morning, before reaching the Dutch border. As the German border guards waved the train across the border, there was a sense of relief from everyone inside. The committee organiser brought round drinks for all the children and offered them a small slice of cake each. She was smiling for the first time since Jan had met her in Danzig.

Unimpeded now, the train moved onwards through the flat landscape of the Netherlands, finally reaching the coast at the Hook of Holland. There, the train stopped right at the water's edge, and they were able to disembark straight onto the ferry platform. They were led up the gangplank onto a small steamship, where they gathered in an open hall area.

"Will we get a cabin?" Jan asked the committee organiser.

"I'm afraid not," she replied, "we didn't have time to organise that – you'll just have to make yourselves comfortable."

Jan looked around – the room had a number of benches positioned at the back and rows of chairs had been set out in front of these. He walked over to one of the benches – at least this might be comfortable, he thought to himself. The two girls from the train were sat on a bench just along from him – one of them smiled as he walked past but then quickly resumed talking to the other.

Jan was excited about being on a ship – he had travelled on pleasure boats before but never on the open sea. As he watched the land slip away though, he suddenly had an appreciation of the distance between him and his parents. It was one thing taking a long train journey, but the sea felt like a real barrier. He blinked away a few tears and tried to imagine what England might be like.

The crossing was quite choppy and many of the children felt seasick. They were encouraged to stand on the deck and breathe in the sea air to feel better. As he watched, one of the girls from the train leaned over the rail and was sick down the side into the water. Jan shuddered and felt glad that he appeared to have a stronger stomach.

In the late afternoon, they sighted land and the ship slowly eased into a harbour, at the mouth of a large river. There was a big, red brick building alongside the quay where the steamship tied up. As they were led off the ship, Jan noticed a sign saying 'Harwich'.

"Are we in England?" he enquired.

"Yes, we are – you're safe now," the committee lady smiled at him.

Jan felt pleased to have arrived but very uncertain about what was to happen to him next. He found himself on a bus with some of the other children, being taken with their bags to a holiday camp nearby. This was to be no holiday though – the camp was full of other refugee children, either waiting to be found foster families or to be sent to their pre-arranged ones. They were housed in the wooden holiday camp chalets - four to a chalet and with adults supervising groups of 3 chalets.

Jan was only in the camp for 2 days before being placed on a train from Harwich station, bound for London, along with 3 other children. On arrival, the camp supervisor who they had travelled with, handed him over to an official looking lady at a stand on the platform. There were other groups of children waiting too and soon he was introduced to Mrs Tubbs, who smiled warmly at him and invited him to call her 'Mama'.

As Mama led Jan out of the station building and waved down a red bus, he stared around at the tall buildings and thought how much it reminded him of home in Danzig. This adventure didn't seem too bad so far.

12

Release Day

Stan looked at the queue ahead of him – there were only about half of the children there had been at the start of the week. He had been in the camp for a fortnight now and could count on one hand the number of faces he still recognised as coming on the same Kindertransport journey as he had done. It seemed that every day children left to go to their new foster families, but he remained. As the clouds of war gathered, Stan had the distinct feeling that he might have been forgotten.

The queue slowly moved - the ladies serving breakfast handing over bowls of hot porridge to each child in turn. When he got to the front and put his hand out, he wasn't surprised to see the daily greyish, slightly congealed offering in the bowl in front of him. It always tasted alright but didn't really look that appealing.

Moving away from the counter, he made his way to a table near the window. He liked to look out across the shingle beach and pretend that he was on holiday here, rather than waiting for something to happen. As he set the porridge down on the table, he pulled the heavy wooden chair out to allow himself space to sit down. The room itself was also mostly wooden, like a lot of the camp buildings, and there were splashes of colour hinting at its past as an entertainment space. The heavy curtains at the end probably hid a stage, he supposed, and if he shut his eyes for a moment, he could almost imagine the laughter which would have once rung around the room.

Lifting the spoon to his mouth he began to eat, each warming mouthful giving him energy, if not enthusiasm, for the day ahead. His mind wandered between the cosy illusion of being on holiday and the more mundane reality of the chores he was likely to be given to do today.

He finished the porridge and gulped down the cup of tea which had been placed in front of him by a lady in a blue checked tabard, before rising to return his utensils to the small hatch in the corner of the room. There stood an untidy stack of bowls, most still containing large dollops of the grey breakfast. He added to the pile and turned to leave, slowly walking out through the double doors and into the late summer morning.

As he rounded the corner of the next hut, he was greeted by an old man brandishing a broom. "Here you go, lad – make yourself useful." The man handed the implement to Stan and indicated the tarmac square in front of the huts with a swing of his arm. "That'll keep you busy for a bit."

Stan's head dropped as he took the broom and started sweeping. He crossed the square back and forth in straight lines, collecting little piles of dust and sand to brush into a dustpan when he had finished. It was monotonous work, measured by the regular lapping of the waves on the shore behind the hut. He wished that he could go and sit on the beach for a while but, despite being housed in a former holiday camp, the refugees life was anything but a holiday. The expectation was that food and shelter were given in exchange for work – this was ok if you were only staying for a few days but Stan's two weeks were feeling like a life sentence already.

"Stan?" – a voice at his shoulder startled him from his thoughts. He stopped and looked up – one of the young ladies from the office was looking across at him. She held a beige folder in her hand and seemed impatient. "Are you Stan?" she asked again.

"Yes, that's right," he replied hesitantly – hopefully this wasn't going to turn into some further chores.

"Would you mind coming with me please? There's someone who would like to meet you."

Stan's curiosity was beginning to take over now.

"Someone who would like to meet me?" he repeated. He wasn't sure what to make of this – he didn't know anyone left in the camp, beyond a couple of children from his train journey, and they weren't exactly close friends.

"Come along – we shouldn't keep her waiting," the woman urged.

So, it was a 'her' then, thought Stan. Not that this piece of information helped him to narrow it down at all. He shrugged, leaned the broom against the side of the hut and followed as instructed.

They reached a door at the end of one of the office buildings and Stan stepped inside. There was a further doorway to his left and two women sat inside, either side of a desk covered in files and paper. The woman behind the desk was dressed from head to toe in black and had a small pair of glasses balanced on the end of her nose. She stood as Stan looked in through the doorway – "Ah, Stan, thanks for coming in," she said in a friendly tone, somewhat at odds with her stern face.

The other woman rose now – "It's nice to meet you, Stanislaw," she said quietly, "I'm Mrs Smith. Doris." He looked at her – she seemed to be dressed in her Sunday best, complete with a large-brimmed hat, and smiled enthusiastically.

"Hello," he answered, "please call me Stan –

everyone does." It felt slightly awkward, almost as if the adults were trying too hard – everything was being slightly over-emphasised.

"Stan, would you mind giving us a moment, please?" the woman behind the desk asked. He stepped out into the corridor, closed the door behind him and let his mind wander as to what was happening back in the office.

"So, Mrs Smith, what do you think?" the woman asked, having sat back down in her chair.

"Well, I'm looking for an older child – someone who doesn't require a lot of looking after," Doris explained. "I'm on my own and I work full time, you see."

"Hmmm," replied the woman, then leaned back in her seat and stared hard at Doris. "These children have come through some difficult journeys to get here and left all kinds of terrible situations at home. I need to make sure that you're committed to this."

"Of course. I'm glad to help," Doris found herself saying.

The office door opened again and both women emerged, smiling nervously. "Well, Stan – I have some good news. You're going home with Mrs Smith here. She'll look after you, as it seems increasingly likely that we'll be at war soon."

"How about you get your things Stan?" Doris suggested. "I'll meet you at the gate."

"Ok," replied Stan, swiftly walking away. He wasn't really sure how to feel – he'd been waiting for this day to come ever since he'd arrived at the camp but, now it had all happened so quickly, he was almost shocked at the thought of leaving.

He was back in no time at all – it didn't take long to pack his small, battered suitcase and all he really had was a change of clothes, plus the ones he was wearing.

"Good luck," called the lady from the office, as they turned and walked through the large, blue-painted gates together. As Stan turned to look back at the camp, he noticed a large sign on the fence – it read 'Dovercourt Holiday Camp'. He gave a little snort and turned back towards the bus stop which was conveniently located right outside the gate.

Doris watched him carefully – "Not much of a holiday, I don't suppose?" she remarked. Stan nodded slowly, a wry expression on his face. "Never mind," she continued, "let's get on the bus – it'll take us to the station."

The bus standing at the stop was cream and single deck. There was a sign in the front window which read 'Refugee Reception Centre'. As they watched, the driver turned it around to reveal 'Station' on the other side. Doris climbed the two steps up into the bus, with

Stan following behind. The bus was about half full and the other passengers looked a little bored and eager for the journey to conclude.

Doris chose a seat behind a lady with a green hat and tweed coat. She had been looking nervously around her. Stan slipped into the seat alongside Doris, tucking his case down by his feet.

"How do you do?" asked Doris, leaning forward, and smiling warmly at the woman.

"How do you do?" she answered, "are you helping out at the Centre too?"

"No, I'm afraid not," Doris said, "I'm hosting one of the refugees." She turned to indicate Stan – "This is Stan – I'm taking him back to London with me."

"Oh – well done you," came the reply, "there are some poor children up here who have been stuck in that camp for weeks, waiting for families."

Doris was about to reply but, at that moment, the driver started the engine with a roar. It was at the front of the bus, next to the cab and, now it was running, the whole bus shook with the vibration. The driver shifted into gear and the bus lurched off, rendering any further conversation impossible.

Before long, the bus pulled into the station and the driver turned off the engine. Everyone rose and politely shuffled off in turn. As he stepped through an arch and onto the grey concrete slabs of the platform, the first thing that Stan noticed was the smell of the sea. It wasn't like the salty aroma he had experienced at the camp though - it was slightly fishy and he didn't like it much. He followed Doris along the platform, noticing an overhead sign reading 'London Liverpool Street'. "This is us," she announced, indicating an open carriage door.

After a few minutes, the train pulled out of Harwich station. Doris had handed some tickets that she produced from her handbag to the ticket inspector and Stan gazed out of the window. He didn't know what to expect as no-one had told him much about England since his arrival. For a boy who had grown up in the city, the flat countryside felt alien without the rows of houses he was used to.

Stan turned to Doris – "What is London like?" he asked. He was starting to feel nervous about where he was going to end up. The camp hadn't been much fun, but it had become familiar to him.

"Well, it's big," replied Doris to start with, "I live in Stepney – it's down near the river. My husband was a dock worker so it was convenient for him."

"What does he do now?" enquired Stan, eager to know a little more about his host's family.

"He died," answered Doris sadly. "It was last winter – he slipped on some ice and fell from a crane."

Stan looked down at his lap, uncertain of what to say next. He couldn't remember what it was like to have a family – he had been in the orphanage for so long. "I'm sorry," he mumbled eventually.

"Don't be – I'm ok," Doris assured him, though he was convinced her face said otherwise. She changed the subject and went on to tell him that her son, Charles, had decided to join the merchant navy and was sailing to India on his first voyage. "The 'SS Empire Conveyor'," she said proudly, "I do hope he brings me back some tea." Stan must have looked confused at this point as she added, "They grow tea in India, you know."

After an age of watching farmland passing by the carriage windows, Stan noticed buildings becoming denser. "Is this London?" he asked.

"Yes, it's the outskirts," Doris confirmed. "A few minutes and we'll be at Liverpool Street."

"What happens then?"

"Well, we'll look for a bus and then get you home for some food. How about that?"

Stan nodded happily. It felt good to be back in a city and he was certainly looking forward to some food.

Road To Nowhere

"So - what do you fancy for breakfast?" Emmie turned to Jack as they walked down the street.

"Forget breakfast," replied Jack excitedly. "We're on the road the bus to school goes along now – let's see if we can get on one. We've got money after all."

Emmie looked hopeful at the suggestion – "Ok, let's walk back towards the bridge and see if the buses are coming past the usual stop." They hurried along the road, heads down a bit and trying to blend in.

"Oh no! Look..." Jack said in disappointment. The stop they normally got off at was just before the railway bridge and almost entirely surrounded by rubble, spilling under the bridge from the destroyed buildings on the other side. Another policeman prowled nearby – Jack stopping dead in his tracks as he noticed the man.

"Come on, let's get out of here," hissed Emmie, pulling Jack's arm urgently.

She looked across at him, taking in Jack's slumped shoulders and bowed head. He was feeling as isolated stuck here as she was. "Ok, tell you what," she started, "why don't we go back past the market, jump on the next bus, ride it for a few stops and see what happens? This is the right road, after all."

Jack looked up hopefully – "Are you sure?" he asked.

"Yes, silly, of course I am," replied Emmie, aiming a playful punch at his shoulder. "I want to get home as much as you do. Maybe we'll be back in time for breakfast?"

They crossed the street – it seemed much quieter on this side and only the occasional vehicle went past. There were a few people walking in the same direction and they joined in with the flow, making their way behind the market stalls and trying to keep a low profile.

Emmie jangled the coins in her pocket – they felt cool and firm, and it was good to think that they might represent a chance to get home again. They stopped at the first bus stop they saw and waited nervously, unsure exactly what the two shillings would buy them from the bus conductor.

After a while, they saw a bus in the distance, making its way slowly along the road. The traffic was still light, but the bus seemed to be stuck behind a small car which was trailing a cloud of blue smoke in its wake. As the car passed them, Jack wrinkled his nose – "Urgh, that smells horrible."

The bus reached the stop and slowed to a halt alongside them. Jack and Emmie gratefully climbed onto the step, with its grooved anti-slip surface, and then ascended to the top deck. The conductor was walking down the aisle and, as the bus moved off again, came over to the pair.

"Where to, please?" he asked. His lined face represented a lifetime collecting tickets and had clearly seen every aspect of humanity passing by.

"Shoreditch. Singles, please," answered Emmie.

"That'll be sixpence then," he replied, holding out his hand.

Emmie handed the two coins over and the conductor looked at her curiously, before returning one, along with a handful of copper coins. He wound the handle of his ticket machine twice and passed the two buff-coloured tickets to Emmie.

Once he had moved along the bus, Jack turned to Emmie – "Why do you think he looked at you like that?"

"I guess sixpence is less than a shilling," answered Emmie, looking down at the coins in her hand.

"Well, that gives us some spare for breakfast if this doesn't work," said Jack, cheerfully. They both stared out of the window, looking for the blue painted shop and wondering if anything was going to happen.

The bus carried on down the road, stopping a few times to let people on and off, but there was no blue shop to be seen... Emmie impatiently tapped the metal rail across the back of the seat in front of them. A middle-aged woman came up the steps at that moment carrying a striped shopping bag. She wore a patterned headscarf and stared at them suspiciously as she sat down.

"Shouldn't you be at school?" she said in an accusing tone.

"We're just off to see our mum in hospital first," replied Jack. Their cover story was sounding more natural every time they used it.

The woman nodded and sat back in her seat, turning to look at them every so often. Jack nudged Emmie – "Time to go?" he whispered.

"Not yet," she replied, "let's stick it out a bit longer. She glanced over at the woman, who was now making no attempt to hide her stare. A few stops later, the bus slowed, and the woman got up to leave.

"Phew – I'm glad she's gone," said Jack, as the bus moved off again. "She was paying us way too much attention." He paused – "I don't think we're going to get anywhere useful on this bus though. I was hoping we might see that blue shop but I'm sure it was closer to the bridge. I don't understand why it's not there now though." Emmie smiled thinly in agreement and pressed the bell button to tell the driver that they would be getting off at the next stop. She couldn't shake the fact that it felt like an acceptance of failure. They stood and walked down the stairs, Emmie turning to look over her shoulder out of the upper windows one last time.

As they stepped off the bus, there was no escaping the fact that they both felt devastated. The high of getting some money to attempt the bus journey properly was being followed by a crashing low. The only way they'd been able to imagine getting home was to repeat the steps which brought them here and now it hadn't worked.

Jack sat down on a wall by the bus stop. He was struggling to hold back tears – he could feel himself welling up and, looking up at Emmie, saw that she was the same. "Come here," he said, holding out his arms. They embraced, each one grateful that they had the other, as it felt like they had nothing else in this strange, parallel world.

Once the low point had slightly subsided, their thoughts both returned to food, though more from necessity than hunger – anxiety was putting paid to that. They hadn't eaten much the previous morning – Jan's bread gift had been welcome but quite small when shared between two.

"Let's look for a bakery," suggested Emmie, "we should probably try and stretch the rest of the money as far as we can." Jack looked around – the road they were on had a lot of houses, mostly set back from the pavement behind small hedges and walls.

"Let's try down one of the side streets," he proposed. He was sure that his nose would help them search out some breakfast. He turned in the direction which the bus had come from and pointed – "I think we should head back, rather than further away." Emmie nodded in agreement.

They took the first side road on the right – it looked to be residential still, but Jack was hopeful there would be shops along its length. He looked up at the road sign on the wall of the first house. The black letters painted onto a dirty white background read 'Viaduct Street'. He could just about see a large brick bridge at the end, which he assumed carried the train line.

As they walked along the road, Emmie noticed some birdsong. It was rarely quiet enough in this part of London to be able to hear such things and she enjoyed hearing the happy chirping. Halfway to the bridge, they came to a corner shop – it looked like a newsagent or general store, with tables of household goods laid out in front. "Worth a look?" asked Emmie.

Jack looked at the shop, sniffing the air. "I'm sure I can smell fish and chips," he said with a grin, suddenly hungry again. He went into the shop and emerged a moment later with an even bigger smile on his face. "I was right – just around the corner!" Indeed he was – there was a young boy putting a sign out on the pavement and the delicious aroma of frying wafted through the air.

Jack and Emmie excitedly entered the chip shop to find that there were more chips than fish on the menu. A chalkboard behind the counter had most of the items crossed off but they were able to spend four of their remaining pennies on a large parcel of steaming chips. Jack was salivating as they left the shop – the smell of vinegar mixed with fried potato was almost too much to bear. Unable to resist any longer, the friends leaned against a nearby wall and eagerly devoured the chips.

"Mmm, that was good," said Emmie, as she finished her last mouthful. "I wasn't sure I was that hungry, but I do feel much better for some warm food."

"Totally," agreed Jack, wiping his mouth with some of the chip paper. The disappointment of the morning felt slightly less pronounced now they had eaten. "I still don't know how we're going to get home though. I don't want to be stuck in 1940 for ever."

"No, me either," replied Emmie. She scrunched the paper up into a ball and aimed it at a nearby litter bin, then laughed when it bounced off the rim. As she walked over to pick it up, she had a thought – "Shall we walk down there to the train line? I'm pretty sure there should be a park just beyond."

They carried on towards the bridge, crossing a different road just before it. As they checked for oncoming traffic, Emmie glanced to the left and felt her heart miss a beat. There was a dark figure who looked very familiar, walking along the path next to a metal fence. They crossed the road and Emmie prodded Jack, pointing at the figure further along the pavement. "Hey, look – what's that person doing?" she exclaimed. As they watched, it ducked, dropped a shoulder and wriggled through the fence.

"It looks a lot like that person who ran away from the shelter," Jack replied, his voice rising in pitch slightly.

Emmie turned to face him - "The radio spy? We need to follow him and see what he's up to..."

14

The Radio – Part 1

When they got to the place where the figure had passed through the fence, Jack and Emmie saw that there was a gap - created by one of the metal bars being bent slightly to the side. It was a tight fit, and the bar had a sharp edge to it, but they managed to ease themselves through. After pausing to check that no one had seen them, Jack scanned the scene in front of him.

"It looks like a factory," he observed. There were several low brick buildings, all with broken windows, and the largest building had collapsed at one end, turning to rubble. There was a strange smell in the air – Jack thought it was the odour of chemicals but couldn't be sure. As he continued looking, Emmie spoke up.

"What kind of factory do you think it is? Or was?" she asked. It was hard to tell – the buildings were quite anonymous looking and, apart from the airborne aroma, there was little to suggest its purpose. "I wonder what that person is doing here?" Emmie continued.

"Let's take a look around," suggested Jack. Emmie smiled to herself – he was quite impulsive, despite his vulnerability in uncomfortable situations. "I think we should start in that building over there." He pointed to the nearest structure – it was the smallest, but it had a door on their side which looked to be ajar.

They walked slowly across a gravel yard, weeds poking through in several places, to reach the doorway. Their footsteps crunched on the gravel and Emmie cringed with each step – if they were going to see what the mysterious person was up to then they needed to avoid making any noise.

Reaching the door, Jack put a hand on the handle and tugged it. There was a squeal from the rusting hinges and Emmie put her hand up to stop him.

"Shh!" she whispered, "we really need to be quieter, else we'll give ourselves away." Jack nodded and gently eased the door a bit further open. As soon as there was enough room to squeeze through, the pair slipped inside.

As their eyes adjusted to the light, they could see the building housed a small office. There were several desks and filing cabinets – their drawers open and empty. Glass lay all over the floor from the broken window and a breeze flapped at what was left of a yellowing blind.

"Nothing interesting in here," said Emmie. "Let's

move onto the next building." It was a few metres away from where they were, built at an angle to the first one and the red bricks at one end looked newer than the rest of the walls.

"How about the main bit of the factory next?" suggested Jack, "there's more likely to be things to see in there."

"I think we're better off moving between them, rather than spending too much time out in the open," replied Emmie. "We still don't know who that person is, or what they are doing. There might be others too – better to be safe than sorry."

Jack nodded and they crept across to the adjacent building. There wasn't a door on the side facing them, so they walked around the back, using the wall as cover, to look for a way in. Peering through one of the broken windows, Emmie saw that there was a large, grey roller door on the far side, facing the main factory unit. It was firmly closed and there didn't appear to be another entrance. The building looked to be used for storage – there were racked shelves along its length, filled with tins and boxes. Despite the broken windows, the storage space looked to be less damaged than the office they had just checked out.

"Let's leave this one for now - we can see that no one is there," Jack proposed. He was keen to get into the main factory building, as he felt sure that was where they would find some answers.

"Ok," agreed Emmie – there was no point in climbing through a window and risking cutting themselves if there was nothing to see inside.

They peered around the corner of the storage building and surveyed the route to the larger structure beyond. The right end, as they now looked at it, was completely destroyed – a large crater with a surrounding pile of rubble was all that remained. The other part of the factory seemed intact, though there were several large cracks running in jagged lines through the brickwork.

"We need to stay away from the ruined end," Emmie instructed. "Shall we try that window in the middle? It looks like there isn't any broken glass in it." Jack looked at the window she indicated – it might have been a ventilation opening originally, as it had a metal frame around it, rather than wood.

"Ready?" he asked.

"Always," came the reply. They ducked down low and headed for the window. As they reached it, there was a loud clang. They both stopped, pressing themselves against the wall either side of the opening.

"Was that you?" hissed Jack.

"No – it definitely came from inside." Emmie's heart was beating fast as she strained to hear if any other noises were coming from within the building. She held her breath and listened. Silence. Whatever or whoever had made the noise had either left or stopped.

"Do you think there's more than one person in there?" Jack whispered.

"Only one way to find out - I'm going in," she said, sounding braver than she felt. She lifted herself onto the window ledge, swung her legs over and dropped to the floor inside.

"All ok?" called Jack, quietly.

"Yes - be quick though." Emmie's voice had a slight echo to it from inside the building. As Jack climbed through the window, he could see that they were at the end of a row of large machinery. There appeared to be several vats and a group of other machines which he couldn't identify.

They crouched down and looked around the space. There was definitely some kind of mixing involved in whatever the factory made. There were lots of tins scattered everywhere and, as Jack looked more closely, he could see that most of the machines had splashes of different colours in random places. "I bet this was a paint factory," he said, "that would explain the smell outside."

They were just about to stand up and explore further when Emmie again caught sight of some movement – this time in the far corner, by a metal staircase. She put a hand on Jack's arm to stop him getting up and they watched a figure walk to the top, seem to fix something to the wall and then descend again. They were close enough to make out that it was a boy – a bit older than them and tall, wearing a long dark overcoat. He seemed to have finished whatever he was doing and slipped out of the factory over the pile of rubble at the far end.

"I wasn't expecting a boy," Emmie admitted, "the figure we saw looked like an adult."

"He is pretty tall," Jack agreed, looking worried. "I wonder if the Germans are using children as spies as they're less obvious?" The fear was gnawing at him again – they had to find out and stop whatever was going on - for their own sake as much as anyone else's...

Jack and Emmie waited a few minutes to see if the boy was going to come back, then deciding that he probably wasn't, stood up and edged around the room towards the staircase. It led up to a metal mezzanine floor which ran the length of the building on one side, ending abruptly where the walls had vanished, and leaving a twisted metal edge.

As they reached the foot of the staircase, Jack stopped. "This feels a bit creepy – are you sure about it?" he asked. Jack was brave to a point but benefited from the reassurance of people around him.

"We've got to know," replied Emmie. "If he is a spy

then there might not be anyone else to stop him. Remember – if what he's doing changes the course of the war then home might not be like home if we ever get back."

"How could I forget?" muttered Jack, trying to shake off his concerns. Emmie put a hand on the stair rail and started to climb. The rail felt cold, and she shivered a little – Jack was right, this was creepy.

Jack followed her and they both reached the top of the stairs. The mezzanine looked to have been an office space too, with a few desks and chairs scattered about. There were lots of bits of paper everywhere – looking very much like a giant had picked them up and sprinkled them all over the building. Emmie supposed that was what happened when a bomb went off close by – everything was thrown up in the air and landed in a mess.

They turned their attention to the wall where they had seen the boy fixing something. Nothing looked too out of the ordinary – it was a bare brick wall, with various hooks and fixings on it. There was a light switch and Jack flicked it on – nothing happened. "Not surprising really," he remarked, "I guess the bomb cut off the electricity supply."

There was a fine wire twisted around one of the hooks, which then dangled towards the ground. Looking down, it was joined to a piece of wood. "Let's check that out," Emmie said, excitedly.

They climbed back down the stairs and crouched over the piece of wood. It appeared to have some paper clips attached to it, a razor blade and a pencil. There was also a strange arrangement of a tin can lid balanced on a bunch of nails which were tied together.

"What is it?" asked Jack, his brow furrowed.

"No idea," replied Emmie, "but I'm sure this is what the boy was fiddling with." She reached out to touch the can lid and examine it further when there was a sudden hiss of static. She snatched her hand back in surprise. "It's a radio!" she exclaimed, "he was trying to make a radio!"

"That's what the magazine was for," said Jack, the pieces suddenly falling into place for him. "He must be the spy... He might even be a German!" He got to his feet with renewed purpose – "We have to stop him – you said it might be different in the future if the Germans do well in the war – what if things change so much that we never get born..."

"How are we going to stop him?" Emmie mused. "We need to catch him in the act and find out what's really going on... I mean – is he the spy or did he just find the radio and the magazine?"

15

Air Raid

It was dusk – the sun had fallen low on the horizon and the last deep orange rays were illuminating the small clouds which hung in the sky. It was mainly clear, which Emmie knew meant that it would be a cold night. What she didn't know yet was that clear skies were perfect for enemy bombers trying to find their target.

On the way back from the paint factory, they had stopped at the corner shop that Jack asked for directions in that morning. They bought a loaf of bread to share for their tea – they'd noticed other people in the shop having to present coupons to buy certain foods, but that bread wasn't one of them.

"I think a lot of food is rationed," Emmie whispered to Jack, as they waited in the queue. They didn't want to draw attention to themselves, so observed what other people were buying and avoided products needing coupons. "I don't know where we'd get the ration coupons from," she explained, "so we'd best play it safe with what we choose."

The bread was quite heavy and seemed to be made

with a mixture of white and wholemeal flour. "This is quite chewy, isn't it?" remarked Jack. He was hungry and the bread was filling him up, but it wasn't quite the same as the bread he was used to.

Once they had finished, Jack reached for the matches and lit one of the candles they'd found the previous day. He placed it into the glass jar and balanced it on the ledge at the rear of the shelter. The candlelight flickered over the grey corrugated metal walls, giving a cosy feel to the utilitarian structure.

"We'd better pull the blackout curtain," said Emmie, getting to her feet and tugging the heavy black fabric across the doorway. She hooked the curtain around the curved edge of the door frame to secure it and sat back down on the bunk. "Well, we shouldn't get bothered now," she mused.

They made themselves comfortable on the upper bunks and settled down for the night. It was cold – as Emmie had predicted – and they both slept in their coats, hugging their arms around them for extra warmth.

After about half an hour, the candle had burned away and Jack realised that there weren't any more in the shelter. "I'll go and have another look in that outbuilding," he suggested to Emmie. He got to his feet and started to unhook the blackout curtain.

"Hold on a minute," said Emmie, quietly – "what's

that sound?"

"I don't hear anything," replied Jack.

"No – wait," Emmie hissed. There was a faint droning noise in the air – similar to the buzzing of a bee. Jack peeked out through the curtain - the moon was out and shining brightly, lighting up the houses around with a pale glow.

"What do you think it is?" Jack asked. "Mosquitos?"

"German planes," Emmie answered, her face looking worried in the moonlight. "They're probably heading for the docks – I think we're in for a rough night."

"Do you think so?" Jack was torn between his interest in scanning the sky to try and catch a glimpse of the planes and the growing gravity of their situation.

"Jack – come back in!" Emmie hissed louder this time. "This is real – real bombs, real bullets, real danger."

Jack looked unconvinced but ducked back into the shelter as Emmie had asked. They sat for a few minutes, listening and wondering how close the night's target might be. The droning was getting louder now, and the sound seemed to separate from a single noise into lots of similar noises which formed an angry, menacing cacophony in the sky. Air raid sirens started up too – adding their eerie wail into the terrifying din.

"Look – there's a searchlight!" called Jack. He was back on his feet and had pulled the curtain back a little to see better. Emmie leaned over to look around him – there was a single searchlight beam shining into the sky down near the river. It criss-crossed the sky, looking for the planes which they could tell were getting nearer by the volume of their engine noise.

Suddenly, there was a boom, closely followed by another one. It was the anti-aircraft guns opening up – more joined in, then several other searchlights pointed their beams diagonally into the sky. Jack and Emmie could see small silhouettes of aircraft passing in and out of the searchlight beams as the operators tried to illuminate each plane to assist the gunners down below. The rhythmic explosions of anti-aircraft shells were creating yet more light in the night sky and it was now possible to see what looked like hundreds of planes moving slowly towards them.

A new noise entered the fray now – a low whistling, followed by a dull thump and a bright flash of light. The aircraft were dropping their bombs. Jack reached for Emmie's hand and squeezed it tightly. "Are they coming this way?" he asked in a small voice – gone was the bravado from earlier.

"They'll be aiming for the docks," Emmie replied. If you look at where the bomb flashes are you can see it's down by the river. "They look like they're heading for us but that's because they're flying up the

Thames."

Jack looked up at the closest group of planes – Emmie was right, they were veering away once they had dropped their bombs. "And don't come back!" he said quietly.

After half an hour of bombardment, the droning noise receded as the last of the planes dropped their bombs and turned for home. The searchlights still shone in the sky and there was an angry orange glow coming from the dockland area, punctuated by the occasional loud explosion. Jack and Emmie stepped cautiously outside the shelter onto the damp grass.

"Do you think that's it for tonight?" Emmie wondered aloud.

"I really hope so," agreed Jack. He was feeling better now the planes had gone, and a little uncomfortable about how he had trivialised it before the raid. It certainly wasn't like a video game, which is how he had imagined it would be.

The streets around them were quiet – families were sensibly still in their shelters and there was no traffic in the blackout. On the night air, came a faint recurrence of the earlier droning.

"They're coming back!" said Emmie, pulling Jack down into the shelter. The same pattern as before started – searchlights waving in the sky to locate the planes, the anti-aircraft guns booming and the dull explosion of bombs hitting the city.

Something was different this time though – as well as flying up the Thames, there was another group of enemy aircraft coming in from the north-east. It felt like there were planes flying towards them and from behind them at the same time. The second group of planes also seemed to be aiming for the inferno down at the docks but were finding the air defences on their approach a stern test.

As Jack and Emmie watched from the shelter doorway, a bomber caught in a searchlight suffered a direct hit and disappeared in a huge explosion in the sky. One minute it was there and the next it wasn't. They didn't know whether to be happy or sad – it was one less plane to drop bombs on London, but they were aware that these aircraft were flown by real people, just like them.

Tapping noises started up on the metal roof of the shelter. "It's not raining, is it?" asked Emmie.

Jack turned from his position in the doorway – "No," he answered, "lots of bits of metal are falling out of the sky." He picked one up, then dropped it like a hot potato. "Ouch!" he exclaimed, "they're hot!" The pair realised that the falling metal was the debris from the air battle overhead – fragments of anti-aircraft shell, bullet casings and, Emmie shivered at this point, bits of plane like the one they'd seen explode overhead.

There was a louder roar from behind them, which caused Jack and Emmie to hold onto each other in panic. As they watched, a plane came into sight overhead with one engine on fire. It was lower than the rest of the planes they had seen, and they were able to see the black crosses on its wings and fuselage. The pilot seemed to be struggling to keep it flying in a straight line and, to their horror, a series of objects tumbled from its belly.

"Those are bombs!" Jack just about had time to shout, before there was a sheet of orange flame from the houses across the road, immediately followed by an earth-shattering explosion. Jack staggered back into Emmie as the ground rocked beneath their feet and a great cloud of dust came rolling across the garden. They lay in a heap on the floor for what felt like ages – their ears ringing, and their senses dulled.

After a while, they were aware of the sound of a bell clanging and shouting outside. Jack pulled himself to his feet and helped Emmie up. The aircraft noise had gone and there was a lot of activity in the street. They crept out of the shelter and slowly walked through the garden to see what was going on.

"Oh my…" Emmie put her hand to her face and stopped in shock. Across the road, two houses had totally disappeared and a third was well alight. There was a fire engine – its crew frantically aiming water at the house in an attempt to contain the blaze – and a number of ARP wardens erecting barriers to stop people coming down the road.

One of the wardens noticed the two faces looking at him from the garden. "Oi – you should be inside!" he shouted, "clear off, now!" Jack and Emmie didn't wait to hear any more and quickly retreated to the shelter. The raid was over but, after seeing so much devastation close up, there was no chance they'd manage to sleep. Instead, they sat up chatting, replaying the night through and trying in vain to make some sense of it.

The next morning, standing in the road and surveying the damage, they realised through their tiredness how lucky they had been to escape serious injury or worse. The houses opposite were a mess – the one which had been on fire was now just a blackened shell, the fire brigade obviously unable to save it, and there were just craters, surrounded by rubble, where the other two had stood.

Jack let out a low whistle – "Nowhere is really safe, is it?"

"No," agreed Emmie, "the station is probably safer because it's deeper, but I feel more comfortable in the shelter." She turned to her left and suddenly her eyes narrowed. "Is that the boy from the paint factory?"

she asked, pointing at a figure who was peering at the scene, whilst half hidden by a lamppost.

"Where?" said Jack, following the direction of her finger. Emmie looked again – there was no-one there. Had she imagined it? One thing she knew for certain was that the last thing they needed now was a reason not to call the shelter home...

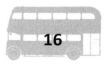

16

Spam Hash

"Who can tell us when the Battle of Trafalgar took place?" Mr Rogers asked the class. The history teacher was a tall, wiry man with thick grey hair, and a habit of peering over his glasses when he looked at them. He was doing just that as he replaced the board rubber and surveyed the rows of desks. Only about half of them were occupied – the result of many children having been evacuated out of London over the past months.

"Anyone...?" he asked again, this time more sternly. A hand went up at the back of the class. "Yes?" he said, hopefully.

"1850, Sir?" came the answer.

"No, no, no," he shook his head, "1805 – can't you remember?" He wrote the year in large numerals on the blackboard and underlined it, as if to cement it in their memories.

Jan sighed to himself – he found it very difficult to be interested in what felt like ancient history in a country which wasn't his own. He liked being in

England but, as for sea battles from over a hundred years ago, he just wasn't feeling it.

Mr Rogers seemed to sense this – he wasn't an unkind man but had a strong desire to ensure all the boys in his class learned everything that he was teaching them. "So, Jan," he started – Jan thought he used his first name as he didn't know how to pronounce his surname - "can you tell us who the Navy was fighting at Trafalgar?" He stood back, hands on hips, looking expectant.

Jan thought hard to himself – it had to be a country with a long coastline, and therefore a large navy. He took an educated guess – "France, Sir?"

"Half marks," came the reply. "It was France and Spain. They had come together under Napoleon in an attempt to control the English Channel."

Jan sat back in his chair. He should have known the other country was Spain – they'd covered it enough over the last few weeks – but his mind had been elsewhere recently, often thinking about adventures he might have with Emmie and Jack.

Mr Rogers wrote 'Events leading to Trafalgar' on the board in white chalk. Jan's heart sank – he knew what was coming next. "Take out your exercise books, please," came the instruction, "I'd like you to write a page on the events which led to the battle and then answer the questions which I'm about to put on the board." He stared at the class, nodding approvingly as books were opened, pens were filled with ink and pencils sharpened.

Jan looked around the room – several of the boys were whispering furtively to each other – no doubt checking what to write. He was sat next to an empty desk – it wasn't uncommon for him to sit alone in the classroom – once the other boys had worked out that he wasn't any good at football, they generally ignored him. He picked up his pencil and began to write - he didn't like the ink pens some of the other boys used as he always managed to get big spots of dark ink on the paper.

"Carry on quietly boys, I'll be back in a moment," announced Mr Rogers, getting up and heading for the door. There was some quiet sniggering from around the classroom – the teacher was well known for needing a 'comfort break' during most lessons and this was no different. As he closed the door behind him, the noise level rose noticeably, and boys started to get out of their seats.

A paper aeroplane whizzed over Jan's shoulder and, as he turned to look, another flew slap bang into his face, hitting him on the forehead. "Sorry!" called a boy who Jan thought was called Johnson, or was it Jamieson? He was never quite sure.

Jan turned back to his paper, trying to concentrate in the midst of a classroom war zone. He'd managed three sentences so far – struggling with some of the more complex words that he had to translate from Polish to English to express himself. He put his head down and carried on slowly.

"Shh – quick, he's coming back!" cried a voice from near the classroom door, where one of the boys was keeping a lookout. The class noisily returned to their seats – boys picking up paper aeroplanes and rubbers to hide the evidence of their distraction.

As Mr Rogers re-entered the room, he surveyed the work on the desks of those at the front. "Is that all?" he muttered, moving along the row. At the end, he straightened and cleared his throat – "This is not good enough, not good enough at all," he said, firmly. "You will all stay behind after school and complete this task to a good standard. No excuses."

Sitting at his desk, Jan groaned inwardly – he was meant to be meeting Jack and Emmie this afternoon and they'd be wondering what had happened to him if he was late. He looked down at his paper – it was almost full – just room for a couple more sentences. He picked up his pencil again and emptied his brain onto the page, quickly scribbling answers to the questions underneath as well.

"Sir?" Jan raised his hand and waited for Mr Rogers to come over to his desk. "I've finished," he explained, offering up the book. Mr Rogers took it and scanned the page.

"The answers are all wrong," he said. "What you've written is good, but you'll have to do the questions again. I can't have you finishing early and everyone else having to stay behind – it would be anarchy." He placed the paper-bound book back on Jan's desk and returned to the front of the classroom.

The clock ticked loudly in the quiet room – it was almost four and the boys had finally realised that the only way out was to complete the exercise they had been set. There was much frantic scribbling and scratching of heads, but it was working – most of them now had at least a full side of writing to hand in. Jan looked down at his page – he'd done the answers again and hoped enough would be right to satisfy Mr Rogers.

At ten past four, the teacher appeared to have had enough – he looked at the clock, pulled out his pocket watch to double check the time, and stood up from his chair. "Alright class, that's enough for today," he declared, "put your books on my desk on the way out." There was a stampede for the door – no-one wanting to stay behind a minute longer than they had to. Jan picked up his bag and followed the crowd – they were probably off to play football but, as usual, he hadn't been asked to participate.

Once outside the school, Jan raced home to get his tea. He was excited to be seeing Jack and Emmie later, and their enthusiasm for his company more than made up for his loneliness. As he reached the house, he saw that Mr Tubbs was just going out.

"Well, hello," he laughed, seeing the boy running down the road towards him. "Where's the fire?!"

"Nowhere, I hope," replied Jan, with a serious look on his face.

"I'm only teasing you, lad," the old man smiled. "I'm just off out for a quick pint – Mama's got your tea in the oven though." Jan's stomach rumbled at the thought of tea and he headed inside to find out what it was.

"Hello, Jan love," Mama greeted him in the kitchen. "How was your day at school?" Jan explained about the history lesson and how he found it hard to relate to what had happened in the past. "Well, it's not surprising," Mama told him, "there's so much going on in the world at the moment – there's not really time to think too much about the past."

"What's for tea, Mama?" Jan asked, hungrily – his eyes on the oven.

"It's Spam hash," she replied, "you'll like it." She opened the oven door and took out a casserole dish with a lid on. Lifting the lid, she wafted it under Jan's nose. He took a big breath – it smelled good. He wasn't the biggest fan of Spam, having been first introduced to it in the transit camp at Harwich a year earlier. It was a greasy, gelatinous substance straight from the tin, but he could just about stomach it when cooked. Mama might be onto something by baking it though – it seemed to change the texture and the aroma was definitely better!

They sat down at the table and Mama put a generous dollop of hash onto the white plate in front of Jan. He stared at it with eager eyes – waiting for her to sit down too so that they could start eating. As they ate, Mama asked Jan about what else he'd done at school that day. He talked about the other lessons – art and biology – but skipped over the rest of the day. It was always awkward admitting out loud that he didn't really spend much time with the other children. He was lonely but preferred to pretend otherwise – focusing instead on what he did enjoy.

Once they had finished, Jan said that he was going out to play with some friends for a while. He was ok with telling Mama this because it was largely true – even though he had only known Jack and Emmie a few days, they felt like friends already.

"Ok – well don't be late and try to be home before it gets dark," Mama told him. She gave him a hug – there was no lack of warmth in the family – as he tugged his coat back on and picked up his cardboard gas mask box.

"Bye," he said, slipping through the back door and pulling it closed behind him.

Once he was out in the street, he turned and headed for the ruined house where he hoped to meet Jack and Emmie. They had an agreement to meet each day, after Jan's tea, and he didn't want them to think that he wasn't coming. It was nice to have some friends for a change and he found the pair quite intriguing. There was something different about them, compared to the other English children that he'd encountered. He couldn't quite put his finger on exactly what it was, but he really looked forward to spending time with them.

He hurried along the city streets, peering into windows as he passed. He often got a glimpse of other families and wondered what was happening in their lives. In some houses, people were already drawing their heavy blackout curtains, even though it was at least an hour until dusk. He supposed it saved them doing it later on when they might forget. Anyone showing a light in the blackout was likely to get a swift knock on the door from the local ARP warden.

As Jan reached the end of the road where the house and shelter were located, he caught the smell of burning in the air. Turning into the road, he could see the temporary barriers that had been erected around the recently bombed houses. He wondered to himself about how bad the damage was.

As he rounded the corner, he stopped dead in his tracks. He could see the craters and rubble where the two houses opposite the shelter garden had once stood. 'Wow – that was so close', he thought to himself. Immediately fearing for Jack and Emmie, he snapped back into action, hurrying across the road and past the debris. He opened the little gate and half ran across the lawn towards the shelter. As he reached it, he could see that the curtain was open and there was no-one inside.

Jan's heart missed a beat – where had they gone? Were they alright? In despair, he called out – "Please come back!"

"Come back from where?" came the voice from behind him. He turned to see Jack grinning at him, with Emmie close behind. They had been in the outbuilding, searching for more candles, and saw Jan arrive.

He ran and hugged them both – "I was really worried about you," he said sniffing. "It looks like you had a lucky escape." He turned his head towards the bombed houses and shivered a little. Even though he'd only know them for a short time, he already felt a connection with the duo.

"Yes – it was pretty scary," admitted Emmie, "but we have something really interesting to tell you..."

The Radio – Part 2

Stan crept down the stairs, one step at a time. He knew to miss the left-hand side of the first three steps because they creaked – still, he held his breath as he trod on them gently. He ran his hand along the worn, striped wallpaper as he descended, idly wondering how long it had been hanging there for.

He reached the foot of the stairs and stepped into the front room. There was an empty bottle of sherry on the sideboard with a glass next to it. Alongside was a picture, lying face down on the wooden surface. He picked it up and stood it back where it belonged. It showed a young man on the deck of a cargo ship – he was smiling to the camera and the ship looked to be far out to sea. He knew the photo was of Charles – Doris Smith's son – and that his ship had been reported sunk in the Atlantic a month ago.

He sighed and backed out of the room. He was hungry but knew better than to expect there to be anything in the house to eat. Mrs Smith, as she preferred to be called, had taken the news of Charles badly, and most days seemed more interested in sitting up drinking sherry than eating. It was ages since she had been shopping – not that there was much in the shops these days apparently – and he was used to fending for himself.

He walked through the kitchen, poured himself a glass of water, and then quietly opened the back door. He pulled it closed behind him and walked the few steps to the passage behind the house. It was better to slip out before Mrs Smith woke and asked any awkward questions about school. She hadn't much interest these days in looking after Stan, nor did she ever have much money, but she was a firm believer in education and wouldn't approve of him skipping school as often as he did.

Stan headed round onto the street in front of the house and walked quickly away, only pausing to pluck an apple from a tree outside the house on the corner. It was light, but only just – the grey dawn breaking in the sky – and Stan hugged his long coat around him to keep warm. He barely saw anyone on these early morning walks – there were a few factory workers coming home after a long shift but most people in their neighbourhood were yet to rise.

As he wandered, Stan thought about life in London since he'd arrived. Back home in Poznan, he'd enjoyed life in the orphanage – he had never known anything else, but it was a carefree environment to grow up in.

The rumblings of war from Poland's neighbour, Germany, had occupied the thoughts of the orphanage staff for a long time before they made the decision to send their charges away. The threat of conflict, mixed with the growing anti-Jewish sentiment being represented in the newsreels, made their decision easier.

When he had first become aware of the enforced emigration, Stan looked on it as a great adventure. He thought the idea of travelling across the sea to a new country was very exciting and the actual journey just heightened his enthusiasm. Sadly, on arriving in England, it became clear that some of the children had foster families already arranged and others, including Stan, did not. They were initially housed in a transit camp – someone said it had been a holiday camp before the war – and the unlucky ones just had to wait it out for someone to take them in.

He had lived in that camp for two long weeks – watching his friends disappear to their new lives – first quickly, and then slowing to a trickle. The camp staff expected the older children to help out with chores and, although this distracted Stan from the sadness at seeing his remaining friends leave, the constant fear of abandonment remained. By the time Doris Smith turned up and was presented with Stan, he was one of only three children to remain from his Kindertransport group.

On that summer morning when he had been called in from sweeping to meet his new foster parent, his first thought was how nice and kind she looked.

By the following spring, things had altered a little – Doris was struggling to make ends meet and had started taking extra shifts at the tobacco factory. Charles had been away at sea for a few months and was rarely home on leave – this made Doris worry constantly and she was, at best, distracted in Stan's direction. When the fateful telegram arrived in August – giving devastating news of the ship Charles was on – Doris retreated into her own little world and shut everyone, including Stan, out.

There was nothing much that he could do – the process which had brought him to England was focused on saving lives by helping children emigrate – not much consideration had been given to what happened after that. He started having to scavenge for food and his declining attendance meant that he fell behind at school. This made it harder when he was there and eventually he decided that the combination of frustrated teachers and slightly hostile classmates wasn't deserving of his time. From this point, he morphed into an accomplished beggar – always trying to avoid stealing food but with desperation driving him on to do whatever was necessary. He was also hugely homesick and longed for news from Poland in order to keep some sort of connection to his homeland.

A truck rumbling past jolted Stan away from his thoughts. It was a dirty green colour and the load bay was filled with a tarpaulin-covered object with various protrusions. He wondered what it could be – drawing level with the truck again as it stopped at some traffic lights. As he gazed at the strange-shaped load, he noticed some rolls of wire laying alongside it. There were half a dozen or so – each tightly coiled and with the end twisted around in a loop to hold them. Realising that they would be perfect for his radio aerial, he quickly looked behind him and then reached over the wooden side and picked up one of the coils. He stepped smartly away from the truck and was just tucking the wire inside his coat when he heard a shout.

"What do you think you're doing?" called the driver, swinging his door open and stepping out in front of Stan. "I saw you take that wire!"

Stan dodged sideways, almost losing his footing on a pile of leaves at the side of the pavement. He started to run, but the man grabbed at his shoulder and he stumbled, nearly falling again. In what could have passed for a comedy hall dance routine, Stan managed to stay on his feet, jinking this way and that, between trees on the pavement. He could hear the truck driver's feet pounding behind him but, when he risked looking over his shoulder, saw that the gap between them was widening.

After what felt like an eternity, he saw a narrow opening between two buildings and raced into it. There was a metal fire escape on the left and he ran up the stairs – two at a time – before changing direction and dropping down into the next street. Fighting to slow his breathing, he forced himself to walk at a normal pace and not look behind him.

When he was satisfied that he was no longer being followed, Stan sank down onto a wall and examined his prize. The roll of wire was shiny silver and about as thick as a pencil lead. There was plenty of it and it would suit his purpose just fine. He tucked the coil back inside his coat and stood up. As he looked around, he realised that the street he was in was unfamiliar and he wasn't sure which way to go. It was a wide street, with leafy trees in front of generously sized houses. Metal bins were on the pavement in front of each house and several had milk bottles lined up neatly on their doorsteps.

Stan decided not to go back the way he had come in case the truck driver was still prowling about. He slowly walked in the other direction along the street, looking for familiar landmarks at each junction he crossed. Eventually, he noticed that there was an elevated section of train line running parallel to him and he turned towards it.

Once closer, he was pretty sure that this was the train line which ran past the paint factory. He looked at the morning sun to work out which way was east and followed the line in the same direction. It ran above and behind a row of houses and then dropped back down to surface level. He read a street name from a sign up high on the end house. "Somerford Street," he said aloud to himself, nodding as he realised he was heading in the right direction.

A few moments later, he was ducking through the gap in the metal fence and cautiously making his way towards the factory building. He skirted the storage shed and headed for the main structure. Clambering over the rubble at the damaged end of the building, he dropped down onto the factory floor, then paused to look around. Everything seemed as he had left it - the wire stretching up to the mezzanine floor and the homemade radio at the foot of the staircase.

He quickly walked across the floor, feet crunching on broken tiles, before clambering up the stairs and taking the roll of wire from inside his coat. He undid the end and wound it around the hook high on the wall, removing the old wire as he did so. This new stuff was much thicker than the old wire and would hopefully work better as an aerial. Once safely attached, he dropped the coil to the floor, watching it unravel as it fell. He followed it down the stairs and then attached the end to the radio.

He had been really excited to find an old magazine

in Charles's room months before, which had an article on how to build your own radio. Initially, he had thought it beyond him but, after reading the article several times, realised the steps were quite straightforward. It had taken several weeks to find all of the materials but, just as described, it had proven possible to build a working radio from everyday objects. It was a shame that he had dropped the magazine a few days earlier when he had been surprised in the Anderson shelter – if any changes were needed to the radio then he would have to guess how to do them.

He stood back and observed his handiwork – it wouldn't ever win any prizes for design aesthetic, but he knew it worked – or at least made a noise. He had struggled with the reception, but the new wire should solve that nicely.

Stan bent down to the radio and started to adjust the tuning but, as he did so, he heard a noise outside. It sounded very much like footsteps crunching over the gravel behind the factory. Fearing that he and his radio might be discovered, he got to his feet and silently crept to one of the shattered windows. Ducking down below the ledge, he listened hard and heard the footsteps again. They were around the side of the building now, so he crept to the end and slipped out under a roller door which stood half raised.

Without looking back, Stan slowly and purposefully

walked towards the fence, keeping the building between him and where he'd heard the noise. As he wriggled though, he risked a look back towards the factory, just in time to see three figures emerge from round the corner and walk through a side door. Pulling his coat around him, he sighed with relief for the second time that morning.

The Paint Factory

"So – what did you want to tell me?" asked Jan excitedly. He had a big grin on his face now he knew that his friends were safe. "Have you found somewhere new to play?"

"No – better than that," replied Emmie. "We think we might have found a spy's hideout!" They had talked together on the way back from the factory and the conclusion they kept arriving at was that the radio must belong to a spy and that the boy they'd seen was involved somehow.

"Could other children have made it and the boy just found it?" Emmie had asked. Jack had thought not – how would they know how to do something so complicated? "I guess the magazine he dropped in the shelter is pretty conclusive," she agreed.

"Are you sure it's a spy?" Jan quizzed them. "I mean – how do you know?"

"Well, we saw that person who dropped the magazine in the shelter again and followed him. He went into a bombed-out factory and, when he'd gone, we discovered a hidden radio," explained Jack.

"Not exactly hidden," Emmie reminded him, "it was in plain sight."

"Yes, but the place was pretty inaccessible," argued Jack.

"Can you show me?" suggested Jan, keen to break up the friendly disagreement.

"Yes – I think there's time to get there and back before it gets dark," agreed Emmie, as Jack muttered something about not wanting to be stuck there forever. "If it is a spy, we need to do the right thing and stop him," she said. Jan nodded in agreement, though he couldn't possibly know just how personal Jack and Emmie's motivation was.

As they walked back out of the garden and past where the houses opposite had stood, Jan shuddered. "Were you here when that happened?" he asked. "It must have been really scary."

"Yep, we were in the shelter watching the whole raid," answered Jack. "It was quite exciting seeing it all happen from a distance. Just like I've seen in pictures at school."

"Pictures?" replied Jan, "what do you mean?"

Emmie quickly cut in here – "Photographs in the newspapers – showing searchlights in the sky and that sort of thing." Jack breathed a sigh of relief – he'd nearly said too much. Jan was their friend, but could they trust him with their biggest secret?

Emmie carried on the explanation – "We watched the bombs drop down by the river and then there was this plane which came over on fire – it dropped its bombs just over the road."

Jan let out a low whistle – "That was close," he said.

"We could see the markings on the plane and everything," added Jack, "it was that low."

"I wonder where it crashed?" Jan mused, "if it was on fire then I doubt it got home."

They got their answer a few streets later – on a patch of waste ground, behind a row of houses, there was a thin plume of smoke spiraling into the sky. As they reached the end house, they could see the remains of a plane smouldering on the ground. The wreckage was partly hidden by the deep furrow it had made on impact, but it was possible to make out the tailplane and cockpit sections – both sitting at unnatural angles. The twisted remains of the metalwork looked like the skeleton of a monster sticking up out of the earth.

"That must be the plane we saw," said Jack quietly. They stopped to stare at the scene and noticed that a small crowd had gathered. Near the plane, an ambulance stood with its doors open and there were two men in overalls holding a stretcher close to the remains of the cockpit.

"Do you think they're trying to get the pilot out?" asked Jan. "No one can have survived that – can they?"

"Fried to a crisp, I reckon. Serves them right anyway – dropping bombs on us..." The three of them looked round and saw a middle-aged woman, hands on hips, talking angrily.

The semi-circle of watchers fell silent. Quite a few people lowered their gaze and shuffled awkwardly.

"How many of us have lost people, houses, livelihoods...?" the woman carried on. There were a number of muttered comments from those around her. "Good riddance, I say," she finished.

"That's not right, Rita," said the woman to her left, firmly, "have a heart - he was somebody's son."

Several other people in the crowd murmured their agreement at this last comment. As they watched, the stretcher bearers lifted something out of the hole and onto the stretcher. They quickly covered it with a sheet, picked up the stretcher and carried it to the ambulance. As the vehicle bumped away across the uneven ground, the crowd started to disperse.

"Come on," prompted Emmie, "if we're going to get to the factory then we need to move." She turned away and started to walk along the pavement, with Jan at her side. Jack, meanwhile, couldn't stop staring at the wrecked plane. It had seemed so distant to start with – watching the air raid with the planes in the sky and the guns firing, but then it had become awfully real. First, the houses across the road disappearing and now an actual dead pilot. A second earlier and Jack knew that the discarded bombs would have landed right on top of them.

"Jack!" called Emmie, "what are you doing?" He finally tore his eyes away from the scene and went to catch them up. He didn't want to walk too quickly as his eyes were full of tears. Struggling with his emotions, he blinked them away as he got closer to his friends.

They arrived at the fence surrounding the paint factory and, after walking past the gap once to check there was no-one about, crouched and scrambled through. There was a chilly wind blowing through the site and little gusts swirled about, picking up dust and grit. Jack and Emmie led the way, walking across the site to the main factory building.

Jan looked about as they walked – "So, what happened then?" he asked.

"We were walking along the other day and saw a figure in the distance who looked like the person we disturbed in the shelter," explained Emmie. "We followed them in here and saw it was a boy – a bit older than us."

"I wonder why he chose here?" Jan looked excited at the prospect of finding out more.

"It's quite deserted – I don't suppose many people come looking around here," Jack replied.

"That building is pretty badly damaged," observed Jan, looking at the largest structure in front of them. "Is it safe?"

"We've kept away from the damaged end – what we're going to show you is on the other side," Emmie reassured him. She led them round the corner of the building and in through a side door. As they entered, something caused Emmie to look across the site towards the perimeter. She was sure there had been some movement by the fence but, when she blinked and looked again, there was definitely no-one there.

They paused inside the doorway as their eyes adjusted to the gloomy interior. Everything was covered in a layer of dust and debris, although there was a maze of footprints criss-crossing the floor which made it hard to tell how many people had been there recently.

"What kind of factory was it?" Jan asked them, looking at the undamaged bits of machinery closest to them.

"We figured it probably made paint," Jack explained, "look around some of the machines and on the floor — there are lots of different coloured splashes."

"Plus, we explored one of the other buildings and that seemed to be a storage shed with lots of tins in — probably paint tins," added Emmie.

They walked through the machine hall towards the mezzanine and staircase. "So, what was the boy doing in here?" Jan asked.

"He was fiddling with that," said Emmie, pointing at the handmade radio on the floor. "It's the radio we told you about."

"That's a radio?!" asked Jan, incredulously. "It looks like a few bits of metal nailed to some wood."

"It's definitely a radio," Jack confirmed, "listen to this." He bent down and touched the tin can lid as Emmie had done previously. As his hand closed around the lid and taped bunch of nails, there was a hiss of static — just like before. "See?" Jack said proudly. He pulled the magazine from the shelter out of his bag and opened it — "Look, this must have been what he used to do it."

"So, does this mean the boy is a spy?" Jan said slowly. "Aren't spies usually a bit older?" He scratched his head and looked confused.

"We don't really know how old he is," offered Emmie, "he looks like a boy, but he could be older." She gestured at the radio — "This is serious though — I mean, why would someone make a radio if they weren't a spy?"

"I guess we don't know for certain that he made the radio" – Jack spoke up. "He could have found it, along with the magazine."

"I suppose so," conceded Emmie. She was getting excited by the possibility that they had found someone up to no good and didn't really want to let go of the idea. There was also the need to preserve the future as it currently was, in the hope that they managed to get home.

"Shall we have a look around and see if we can find anything else which might explain how the radio got here?" suggested Jan. Without waiting for an answer, he started up the staircase next to them.

"Jan – be careful!" warned Emmie, "we don't know if there are other people involved in this." She had also remembered that the mezzanine ended abruptly at the damaged end of the factory and hurried after him, concerned that he might fall in his excitement. Luckily, Jan was searching through the drawers of the desks – most of them were open already, their contents scattered across the floor. He moved between the various desks, trying to look methodically.

Most of the undisturbed desk drawers were empty. A few had files with sheets of paper in them and the odd pencil or eraser, but there was nothing really of interest. Jan stopped at one drawer which appeared to be locked – "Help me open this?" he asked.

Jack walked over and the two of them wiggled and jiggled the drawer, trying to release the lock. It was no good - the desk was solid, and the drawer wouldn't budge. Exasperated, Jan gave the desk a shove.

'Clink.'

"What was that?" asked Emmie, coming over and looking down at the floor in front of the desk. Glinting in the fading sunlight from one of the roof windows, lay a small silver key. "Someone must have hidden the key under the desk and it fell down when you knocked it," she suggested.

Jan eagerly picked up the key and put it into the drawer lock. It turned and he slid the drawer open. It was empty. "Huh!" he said, "why would anyone lock an empty drawer?"

"Have you checked this cupboard?" called Jack, who had wandered over to the other side of the mezzanine. He rattled the door handle and the cupboard creaked open. Inside, on a shelf, lay some screws, a screwdriver and a roll of wire. "Look – it's things left over from the radio – the boy must have made it!"

"How do we know that another person didn't make the radio and leave this here?" Emmie said. "It doesn't prove anything, unfortunately. He might have found the magazine or be keeping it for someone else."

"Well, we need to find that boy and see what he gets up to then," announced Jack, "then we'll know if he's a spy or not."

"Shall we wait it out tonight?" Emmie looked at them in turn, "he might come back."

Jan shifted awkwardly on his feet – "I really need to get home," he said, "Mama will be worried – it'll be dark soon." He was conflicted – he really wanted to know what the boy had been up to and didn't want to miss out on the adventure, but also knew he'd be in trouble if he wasn't home soon.

Emmie sensed this and smiled at him – "Tell you what, why don't we meet tomorrow after school and come to have another look? He might be here then."

Jan looked relieved – "Oh yes please, that would be great." Now he could be included and still get home on time.

As they walked out of the factory, squeezed through the fence and began the trek home, Jan smiled – it was great having friends and he had a feeling this adventure had only just begun.

Jack looked at Emmie, who was deep in thought – this spy thing was playing on her mind – first the figure in the shelter and then the boy at the factory. They were definitely the same person but how involved with the radio were they? Was it safe to go back to the shelter – would he go back there?

A Real Spy?

The next afternoon, Jan rushed out of the classroom with uncharacteristic speed. He usually took his time packing up his bag and was in no hurry to join the crush of other pupils in the school corridor. To the surprise of his teacher, he took off like a shot the moment the bell rang for the end of class.

As he skipped down the steps leading to the front entrance, Jan's mind was racing with possibilities of what they might find at the factory today. He had told Mama that he would be late home for tea – the cover story was that he and some friends were building a den in the park. She had agreed happily – it had taken a long time for Jan to talk of friends and she knew this was a big part of his childhood that had been missing.

Walking briskly across the playground, its surface covered with the markings for hopscotch and other school games, he craned his neck to see if Jack and Emmie were waiting. They had said they would be outside after school so there would be maximum daylight for exploring. He passed through the gates and scanned the road outside – they weren't there.

Deflated, he walked on a bit and then saw them waiting by a hedge, around the corner from the school. He waved excitedly and crossed the road to join them.

"How was your day at school?" asked Jack. He was carrying his schoolbag and Jan could see a bulky torch sticking out of the side.

"Fine, thanks. How is your mum?" Jan chatted eagerly as they walked away from the school together.

"Mum's a bit better, thank you," Emmie chimed in. They had to keep reminding themselves where they'd got to with the story of their fictitious mother so that it appeared real still.

Jack patted his bag – "I found a torch," he explained. "It was in the outbuilding – right at the back." He went on to say that there were no spare batteries so he hoped it would last during their exploration that afternoon.

As they proceeded down the road, Jan talked about the rest of his day. He really liked having people to share his experiences with – he'd been lonely for a long time since arriving in London and, although Mama always asked about school, it was great to talk to people his own age too. Jack and Emmie got to hear all about how much Jan enjoyed art and maths but thought history a little pointless. "Especially English history," he joked, "I am Polish – why would I need to worry about that?"

Soon, they passed the chip shop that they had stopped at a few days before and Jack spent some of their precious remaining pennies on chips for tea. They stood leaning against the wall outside, sharing the chips and listening to Jan's theories about what they might find in the factory today. "There could be a whole group of spies having a meeting," he suggested, excitedly. "Or maybe we'll find a code-book?" Emmie smiled outwardly as Jan talked – she was still spooked by the idea of a spy in their midst but determined to do whatever it took to stop them from succeeding in their mission, even if it distracted from the immediate ability to get home again. It was essential to ensure that home was as they'd left it before they tried to get back.

As they arrived at the factory fence again, Emmie felt a fluttering feeling of apprehension in her stomach. Was something wrong or was she just thinking too much? She paused at the gap in the fence, half tempted to suggest they called this escapade off, but then realised that she had nothing tangible to offer as a reason. Gritting her teeth, she ducked through the gap and then stood aside so Jan and Jack could follow.

Glancing around the site, everything appeared as it had the day before. The air was still, and the bomb-damaged buildings looked deserted. There were a couple of blackbirds flying about, which felt like a good sign there weren't any people present.

Jack took the lead – he and Jan started across the broken ground between the fence and the first building, with Emmie following and trying to shake off her worries. They entered through the side door as before and headed over to the foot of the stairs. The radio was still in the same place and didn't look to have been touched.

"Not quite the grand meeting of spies you had in mind," Jack joked to Jan.

"No," he agreed, "let's look around again though – we might still find something."

They ascended the metal staircase, their shoes making a dull ringing sound on each step. At the top, Jan headed for the cupboard that they'd found the equipment in. "It's gone!" he said, with a mixture of surprise and disappointment. "Did we leave the cupboard open yesterday?"

"I don't think so," replied Emmie, "we've been trying to leave things as we find them."

Jan carefully searched every corner and crevice in the cupboard to see if anything else was hidden in there. "Nothing..." he said sadly, after a few minutes of rummaging.

Emmie sat down on one of the desks - "Well, I think the boy must have been back and collected his stuff. He might even have been watching us and crept in when we left."

"Do you really think so?" – Jan wasn't sure if he was more annoyed at missing the boy's return or excited at the idea that he'd actually returned. "If he's been back once, then I'm sure he'll come again," he said optimistically.

They spent another half hour working through all the possible hiding places on the mezzanine floor. There wasn't much furniture left so it hadn't taken long, though they had flicked through all the paper scattered around to make sure there wasn't anything that looked like a secret code in amongst it.

"There's nothing else here," announced Jack. "We could wait like you suggested yesterday but there's no telling when he might come back." Just then, the decision was made for them as it started to rain. The broken windows in the factory roof meant that the rain came straight through and splashed around them on the floor.

"Come on then," suggested Emmie, "let's get out of here before we get soaked."

They ran out of the building laughing to each other in the rain. It was one of those silly moments where everything seems funny – Emmie was dancing around and the boys were shouting up at the sky – "Come on, rain harder – dare you!" The rain seemed to oblige and, after a while, they realised that getting wet wasn't actually that much fun after all. Jack led the way over to the fence and they ducked through the gap, staying close to the wall which joined it, in order to stay a bit drier.

The rain didn't show any signs of abating and the trio rushed along the pavement to take shelter under a nearby tree. The tree still had a covering of leaves, despite the lateness of the season, and it stopped the worst of the droplets cascading from the sky.

"What next?" asked Jan, taking his glasses off to wipe them. He had then put his hands into his coat pockets and found that they were sodden – "I'm cold and not enjoying the rain anymore."

"Me either," agreed Emmie. She squeezed the water out of her hair and shook the plaits to dry them a little, thinking wistfully about home with its hot shower and hairdryer. It looked slightly brighter on the horizon now and she hoped they would be able to make it back without getting any wetter.

A car trundled past them, windscreen wiper moving slowly from side to side across a fogged-up screen. It was close to the kerb and, as it passed them, a big splash of water flicked up from the gutter and landed next to Jack's feet.

"That was close!" he exclaimed, "let's move before it happens again." He strode purposefully out from under the tree, looked up at the sky as if to challenge it, and then called over his shoulder – "What are you waiting for?"

Emmie and Jan followed – it wasn't raining that hard now and at least they were moving in the right direction. As they passed along quiet streets of houses, Emmie wondered when they might see normality again. The longer they were stuck in 1940, the less likely it seemed that they would find a way to get home.

"You look sad," observed Jan. He turned to look at Emmie as they walked along – "Are you worried about your mum?"

Emmie hesitated for a moment – there was such a lot to keep secret and it would be good to be able to talk to someone else about it. Surely no-one would believe their story though - not even nice, kind Jan. "Yes – that's it," she agreed, trying to force a smile – "we went earlier and she was getting better. She's in the right place to be looked after."

Jan nodded and continued – "That's good. So, what do you think we should do about the radio? Should we go to the police?"

Jack turned and looked alarmed. Emmie quickly answered – "No, I don't think we should do that yet – maybe we can go back tomorrow and stake the factory out to see who comes?"

"Good idea – it's Saturday tomorrow so we'll have all day," Jan said happily.

They soon found themselves at the end of the road to the shelter house. "Want to come and explore the outbuilding again?" Jack suggested to Jan.

"Yes please," he replied. There hadn't been much time to look around before, as it had been getting dark, but today there was more daylight left.

They walked up the garden quietly – Emmie breaking off towards the shelter. Jan and Jack went to open the outbuilding door, when suddenly there was a loud shout. "WHAT ARE YOU DOING??!!" They spun around to see a figure emerge from the shelter entrance with Emmie hanging onto its coat sleeve. As she twirled them around, Jack could see that it was the boy from before. He started to run across the grass but, before he could get there, Emmie had dragged the boy to the ground and was sitting on his chest.

Jack arrived as the boy was desperately twisting and turning, trying to knock Emmie off. "Stop!" she said, but it was no good – he kept writhing around in an attempt to unseat her. Jack reached down and grabbed his shoulders to stop him moving so much.

The boy shouted a word that they didn't understand – he was fighting the two of them to get free now.

"See – he is a spy!" shouted Jack, "he's talking German!"

Jan had been standing by, staring in horror at what was going on. "That's not German," he said slowly, "it's Polish!"

He leaned down next to the boy and said some words quietly to him. Immediately, he stopped struggling and stared at the trio. "You can get off him now," said Jan.

Jack let go of the boy's shoulders and Emmie stood up, brushing down her skirt. The boy sat up and pushed himself back a little way, so that he was no longer in the middle of them.

"Does he speak English?" asked Jack.

"Yes," replied the boy, "I do."

Everyone started talking at once then – all asking questions, which made the poor boy's face screw up in confusion. Emmie took charge – "What's your name?" she asked.

"I am Stan," he replied.

"That's not a very Polish name."

"My real name is Stanislaw – everyone calls me Stan – it's easier," he explained.

"What are you doing here? This is our shelter."

"Your shelter? But the house is ruined," Stan said, with a little uncertainty in his voice.

"We've been staying here," interrupted Jack, "and now you're trying to steal our things."

"I was just looking for a place to sleep," protested Stan, "it's really cold at night."

"That's not true - and we know that you're a spy!" Stan looked shocked and Jack smiled triumphantly – "And now we're going to fetch the police..."

20

The Truth, The Whole Truth & Nothing But The Truth

"No, no, no, please no," begged Stan, his eyes big and scared. He pushed himself further away from them, his back now almost touching the earth bank of the shelter.

"Yes – you're a spy all right – we found your radio!" Jack sneered as he spoke. He pulled the magazine out of his bag and held it up – "And you dropped this too – how do you explain that?"

Jan looked confused in the middle of all this – he was caught between his friends and this strange Polish boy who he felt an immediate protective bond with. He had never set eyes on him before but yet was drawn to help him. "Shall we let Stan tell us what is going on?" he said quietly.

Jack looked at Emmie, who nodded in agreement. "Come on Jack – it's only fair," she urged. She turned to Stan – "Ok then, what's going on?"

Stan looked nervously around the group and tried to move even further back. "That's far enough," Jack glared at him. "You're not going anywhere until we get an explanation."

The boy cleared his throat and spoke in a low voice – "I was looking for somewhere to shelter," he started. "It was raining, and I was trying to stay dry."

"Where do you live," asked Jan, gently. He stepped closer to Stan – "Don't worry, I just want to help."

"I live with a lady, but she isn't there much," explained Stan. "Her son died and she's not coping." He went on to explain about Mrs Smith and how she had come to the refugee camp and brought him back to London.

"You were in that camp too? In Harwich?" asked Jan in surprise. "I was there last year. I only stayed for 2 days before coming to London."

"You were lucky," Stan said sadly – "I was there for 2 weeks. I watched almost all of the other children I travelled with leave."

"Didn't you have a host family arranged? My parents chose one for me before I left Danzig." Jan looked a little confused at the thought.

"I lived in an orphanage – a Jewish one – and the people there were so keen that we got away before the Germans invaded that they sent us without arranging hosts." Stan said all of this in a matter-of-fact way, but the others were staring open mouthed at him.

"That's really sad," Emmie offered, "being sent away from your home without knowing where you were going or who to."

"He still hasn't explained about the radio..." muttered Jack. He wasn't ready to accept Stan's story whilst there was still suspicion about his motives.

Emmie turned to Stan – "Ok, so what about the radio?" she asked. "We know you're hiding one – why?"

Stan looked scared – "I... I don't know what you mean..." he stammered. "I was just looking for somewhere to shelter – like I told you."

Emmie frowned – "We know about the radio," she said firmly. "We saw you."

"He's lying," Jack said crossly, and took a step towards Stan.

"No," said Jan, stepping in between them. "He's not finished talking yet." He crouched down next to Stan again – "We saw you at the paint factory," he explained. He went on to recount how they had found the radio inside and then realised the significance of the magazine article showing how to make it. "So we know you're involved with the radio somehow," he finished.

Stan sighed and looked down at the grass – "I'm not a spy," he said. "I miss home – Poland I mean. I wanted to hear Polish voices and some news from there."

"Go on," Jan encouraged him.

"I tried to use Mrs Smith's wireless, but it was no good – the furthest station I could find was in France. Then one day Charles went missing... Charles is her son – he's a sailor. I was helping her tidy his things and saw a magazine about radios, so I sneaked in later and borrowed it." He paused and looked up. Emmie, Jack and Jan were listening intently to his story.

"I read the magazine and realised that you could make a radio from things lying around in the home, so I gave it a try. It took a while to get everything I needed but it worked."

Emmie smiled encouragingly – "Did you get to hear any news?"

Stan explained that, although the radio worked, the aerial hadn't been good enough. "So, the other day I found a roll of wire and went to replace it. I haven't had a chance to try it properly though."

"What do we think?" Emmie asked, turning to the others. "It sounds plausible to me."

"Me too," agreed Jan – "I know what it's like to be far from home and wanting to hear some familiar voices."

"Don't we all," whispered Jack quietly to Emmie. "Ok, sorry for calling you a spy," he said in Stan's direction. He then remembered his manners and put his hand out to help Stan up. He hauled him to his feet and handed him back the magazine.

"Thanks," Stan said.

"What will you do now?" Jack continued.

"I guess I'll look for somewhere else to sleep tonight. Sorry for intruding."

"No, wait," Jan put his hand up, "you should stay. It's cold and we're all wet through." Jack nodded vigorously at this comment – he wished he had a warm jumper instead of the thin school blazer under his borrowed coat.

"I agree," said Emmie. "Stan – you must stay. We'll try and light a fire to dry us out."

Jack went to look for anything of use in the outbuilding and came out carrying a metal dustbin. "We can light a fire in this," he suggested. "There's loads of wood in a pile around the back too." He placed the dustbin down on one of the paving slabs set into the lawn and turned to go back.

"I'll help." It was Stan - he looked less scared now and was eager to bond with these new people. "I can carry some wood at least."

"Ok," replied Jack, "thanks." They both disappeared behind the outbuilding and returned with armfuls of logs – split into halves and quarters. Jack placed his haul on the ground next to the dustbin -

"There's enough to keep us warm tonight." Stan followed suit and then began to build a pyramid of wood in the base of the dustbin.

"Is there anything to start it with?" he asked. Jack threw him the box of matches, which Stan deftly caught. Stan then picked up a few thin sticks which had been inside the outbuilding, snapped them into shorter pieces and placed them in the centre of the pyramid. Touching a lighted match to the thinnest stick, he stepped back and watched the flames grow. After a few minutes, there was a good blaze going and the four children gathered round to warm themselves.

"That's better," announced Emmie, who had started to shiver in her wet coat. "We should enjoy this while there's still light though – we'll have to put it out when the blackout starts."

Jack nodded his agreement – "Hopefully we'll be dry by then." He disappeared for a moment and returned with another dustbin. Taking off his coat, he carefully placed it over the new dustbin as if it was wearing it, then moved it close to the fire. "That should speed things up – we can all have a go too."

"Are you hungry?" asked Stan. He hadn't spoken much since he'd lit the fire and had been staring into the flames as he warmed his hands and clothes.

"You bet!" replied Jack and Emmie in unison. The chips they'd shared with Jan seemed ages ago now.

"I'm going to have to get home for tea soon." Jan looked at each of them in turn – he wasn't quite sure how they were going to get on without him there to mediate, but Mama would be expecting him home.

"Stay a few minutes longer? You're still soaked – at least get dry." Emmie looked at him with a concerned expression.

"Ok – a few more minutes," he agreed.

"Did you have a suggestion for getting some food?" Jack asked Stan.

"Oh yes – I wondered what might be left in the house still," Stan replied. "Have you looked?"

"No – we kept away in case it wasn't safe," Jack answered him. "We've eaten vegetables from the garden but there's not much of the house left apart from rubble."

Stan shrugged – "Doesn't look that dangerous to me. I'll see what I can find." They turned to look at the house – there was a small portion of the kitchen still standing at the rear, which had been difficult to see from the road. Most of the house had disappeared into a large mound of rubble but the section they could see, which was on the side of the adjacent semi, had escaped total destruction.

He turned, and without a further word, walked quickly towards the back of the house. They watched as he scrambled over a small heap of rubble and slid into the remains of the kitchen. He ducked down and appeared to be lifting something up.

"Shall I go and help?" suggested Jack. He wasn't keen on being upstaged by the newcomer's bravado.

"No – you really shouldn't," Emmie answered him. "I still think it's dangerous, despite what Stan says."

There was no time for further discussion as Stan came sliding back over the pile of rubble at that moment, carrying some tins proudly. He placed them in front of the others and smiled. "They're a bit dented and seem to have lost their labels but they're still sealed."

"Lucky dip tea then," Emmie said, "well done Stan." She picked up the first tin and shook it. "I can't tell what's inside," she admitted. The others laughed and picked up tins too.

"Any idea how to open them?" Jack looked around for something sharp which might pierce the tins.

Stan put his hand into his coat pocket and produced a penknife. He reached out for Jack's tin, then used one of the attachments to roughly hack the tin lid open. "Looks like soup," he observed.

Jack took the tin back and sniffed the contents. "Oxtail, I think." He placed the tin close to the fire – "Hopefully that will warm it up a little."

Stan then opened a tin for Emmie and one for himself. It really was lucky dip – there was a tin of rice pudding and one of boiled potatoes. He placed the tins next to the first one beside the fire and sat back to wait.

"It's time for me to go now," announced Jan, picking up his coat which had been having a turn closest to the fire. "Will I see you all tomorrow? It's Saturday so shall I come here in the morning?"

Emmie looked at Jack, who nodded, then at Stan. "Stan?" she asked, "we'd really like you to stay."

A small smile played on Stan's lips – it was the first time he'd actually looked happy since they'd arrived. "Thank you," he said, "I will."

Jan looked very relieved at this development. As he slipped his coat on, his face broke into a big grin. "I can't wait for tomorrow," he admitted excitedly. "I'll see you then."

Sitting around the embers of the fire a little later, after having said goodbye to Jan, Emmie asked Stan a bit more about the family he lived with.

"It's just Mrs Smith, now that Charles has gone," he explained. "She was alright to begin with, nice even, but after a few weeks it was like I was an inconvenience." He told them how there was never much food in the house and that he'd started trying to find his own, just to avoid going hungry. "She couldn't really seem to afford to feed herself, let alone me."

"Makes you wonder why she volunteered to look after you in the first place," remarked Emmie.

"I just feel like I don't fit in," said Stan sadly. "The boys in my class don't really like me and it seems like I'm stuck here. I'd rather be at home." He sniffed, then continued – "It's like no-one understands me or what it's like."

Emmie studied his face – he looked utterly dejected. "I understand more than you think," she said softly. "We're not meant to be here either."

"What do you mean?" asked Stan, looking closely at her. Emmie paused for a moment, considering the gravity of what she was about to say and wondering if she should.

"Well, you won't believe this, but we live in the future – we got to 1940 by accident and now we can't find our way home..."

21

Secrets

Stan and Jack both stared at Emmie. Stan's eyes were open wide, and he wore a confused expression – Jack, meanwhile, looked totally shocked. After a long pause, he spoke first.

"Why did you say that, Emmie? I thought we weren't telling anyone?"

Stan looked from one to the other. He couldn't believe what he was hearing, yet the reaction from Jack suggested there was something in it.

"What do you mean?" he asked slowly. "When you say 'the future', do you mean the actual future?" He scratched his head – "How is that even possible?"

"Well…" began Emmie, looking at Jack to gauge his reaction. He nodded slowly – it was actually a relief to finally admit what was happening to someone else. "We don't really know – we were on the bus home from school and there was suddenly a big flash and the ground shook. When we got off, everything looked different, and we got caught up in an air raid."

Stan sat back and chuckled – "Nice try. It's a really

good story. You almost had me fooled for a minute there." He looked at the pair, realising that their expressions were still deadly serious, and the laughter dried up in his throat. "You're not joking, are you?"

It was Jack's turn now – "I wish we were," he admitted. "It felt like a big adventure at first, but now we're stuck in a familiar place but yet far from home. All we really want to do is get back."

"Can't you just get back on the bus?" Stan asked. "If that was how you got here, maybe it's the way back?" He couldn't really believe that he was going along with this crazy story - he knew it wasn't possible to travel through time - but yet there was something compelling about the way Jack and Emmie told it.

"We tried that," explained Emmie sadly, "a couple of times actually, but it didn't work."

"We think there's a shop that's relevant somehow," Jack added, "just before the flash, when we got off the bus, we saw a blue painted shop with a gas mask in the window. I'd never seen it before, even though we get the same bus to school every day."

' "It's very unusual to see things from eighty years ago in shop windows." Emmie's words made Stan's eyes widen further.

"Eighty years? That's a long way into the future... The world must be so different..." Stan was intrigued but still struggling to credit their story as true. That said, a lot of things had happened in the world in the past year which no-one thought previously possible... "Can you tell me what it's like?"

"We've got to be careful," Emmie said, "have you heard of the butterfly effect?"

"No," replied Stan, "what's that?"

"It's the idea that, if you were able to go back in time, you have to be really careful not to change the course of history," Jack chimed in. "We learned about it at school last year."

"Yes," agreed Emmie, "if you accidentally killed a butterfly in the past, then it's possible that whichever creature may have eventually eaten that butterfly for lunch could have gone hungry, died even, and the consequences might grow and grow."

"Even a small change can repeat many times into a bigger change overall," finished Jack. "What we're basically saying is that we can't tell you too much, in case it has an unexpected impact. This is why we were so concerned about spies – if something happened to change the course of the war then our future might be totally different to the one that we've left behind." Stan shivered involuntarily at this point – he knew only too well what that future might be like.

"How do I know that you're telling the truth though?" Stan pondered.

Jack reached for his school bag and rummaged

inside - "How about I show you this?" he suggested. He pulled out his calculator and passed it to Stan, showing him how to turn it on. "Have you ever seen anything like this before?"

Stan turned the calculator over in his hands, staring at the unfamiliar device and touching the buttons. "No," he said, "what is it?"

"It's called a calculator," Jack explained, "you use it to add numbers together." He demonstrated, leaving Stan to play with the gadget in wonderment.

"This is something else," said Stan, after a few moments, "how on earth does it work? It's like magic."

"Well, the sun charges the battery through this little panel here..." started Jack. He stopped, seeing the bewildered expression on Stan's face – "let's just say it's very clever," he finished.

Emmie put her hand to her mouth as she stifled a yawn. "I'm really tired," she admitted. "Shall we put this fire out and settle down for the night?"

They all nodded in agreement – Stan replacing the dustbin lid so that the embers wouldn't be visible – and then retreated to the bunks in the shelter.

As he lay down and tried to get to sleep, Stan reflected on the day. His head was spinning from the elation of finding a wire for his radio, through the shock of being cornered and now the almost unbelievable revelation from Emmie and Jack.

Stan slept fitfully. He never slept that well these days – it was probably as a result of not being in a settled home – tonight had been worse than usual though. He had dreamed of being on the train journey from Poland and then the train had turned into a bus and gone into a never-ending dark tunnel. He had woken up in a sweat and sat up on the bunk – his heart pounding and with goosebumps all over his skin. When he finally got back to sleep, the dawn was breaking, and he could see faint smudges of light coming around the edges of the thick curtain.

"Are you awake, Stan?" came Emmie's voice from the other bunk. She was whispering, so he guessed Jack was still asleep.

"Yes," replied Stan softly. "I didn't sleep too well."

"Sorry to hear that." Emmie was sitting up now, looking across at him. "Do you miss home?"

"Yes, sort of." Stan turned towards Emmie - "The people in the orphanage were nice and I'm just so lonely here."

At that moment, they heard footsteps running over the lawn outside and a voice called 'Hello' – it was Jan. As he poked his head around the blackout curtain, he waved a bag excitedly – "I've got breakfast!" He stepped inside the shelter and produced a small loaf of bread from the bag, along with 3 apples.

"Oh Jan, that's so kind," smiled Emmie, "where did

you find the bread?"

"Mama was baking early this morning," explained Jan, "so I asked if I could have a small loaf to take out for my lunch – luckily, bread isn't rationed."

Jack had woken up by this point, so they all sat on the bunks eating the bread and apples. "How did you get on last night?" Jan asked.

"Well, Jack and Emmie told me their secret – that was pretty much all we talked about," Stan replied.

"Secret?" asked Jan, sounding confused. He felt a sudden wave of sadness – he'd met Jack and Emmie first and there was a secret which they'd not shared with him but told Stan almost at once.

"Oh… I thought you must have known already…" Stan correctly read Jan's expression – "I'm sorry…"

Emmie and Jack glanced at one another, trying to decide whether to let Jan in or not. Maybe it had been a mistake telling Stan the truth but, then again, they could do with as much help getting home as possible. Jack nodded at Emmie, who then turned to Jan and looked him right in the eye. "Jan – we told Stan last night that we're not from here – we're from the future. We were on the bus home from school and somehow we ended up in 1940."

Jan's face went from shock to disbelief as Emmie spoke. Surely they were making this up to cover for the fact that they had told Stan their real secret. He blinked back tears – "I thought we were friends," he sniffed. "Couldn't you trust me with your secret, whatever it is?"

Emmie tried a smile – "It's the truth, Jan. We weren't going to tell anyone as it doesn't sound very believable but, hearing Stan's story last night and how he is longing for contact with home, it just slipped out. We feel exactly the same – trapped here without knowing how to get back."

Jan blinked – he wanted to believe Emmie, she was his friend after all, but from the future – how was that possible? "How did you get here?" he asked slowly, "what happened on the bus?"

Jack picked up the story, recounting how they'd seen the antique shop with the gas mask in the window and then, as they'd stepped off the bus, experienced a bright flash and a loud bang.

"Sounds like a bomb going off," remarked Jan. "Were the flash and bang after you'd got here or before?" He checked himself – he'd asked the question like he believed the story. Did he? It was impossible, wasn't it? However, it would go some way to explaining why the pair seemed different to everyone else.

"I don't know," admitted Jack, "it all happened so fast. We didn't notice that anything was different until we ran into the Tube station to shelter from the rain. Even then, Emmie wondered if we'd stumbled into a film set."

"What do you mean?" asked Jan. "A film about the war?"

"Exactly," Jack replied, "we thought that the station might have been made to look like 1940 for a film."

"And all the people were actors," added Emmie. "It was only when there was an air raid and we were stopped from leaving, that it started to feel real."

"That, and the next morning when we saw some of the buildings outside the Gardens had been destroyed," Jack concluded.

"What do you think?" Jan turned to Stan, who had been sitting quietly up to this point.

"I couldn't believe it either," he replied, "I mean — time travel isn't possible, is it? Then Jack showed me his adding up gadget and that can only have come from the future — I've never seen anything like it before."

Jack pulled the calculator out of his bag and handed it to Jan. Emmie leaned over and showed him which buttons to press. Jan's eyes bulged — they were right, he'd never seen anything like this either. "What do you use it for?" he asked.

"Adding numbers up at school," replied Jack. "It saves loads of time."

"I bet it does," Jan said, "does everyone have one?"

"Yep – right from primary school," Jack confirmed.

Jan sat back – this still seemed really far-fetched, but the calculator was clearly from somewhere more advanced. "Ok," he said cautiously, "what are you planning to do next?" He wasn't sure that he wanted to hear the answer – just as he had found some friends it looked like they weren't planning to be around for long.

Emmie answered – "Well, we've tried to get on the same bus journey again a couple of times in an effort to get back, but it hasn't worked. We're not really sure what to do next."

"Have you found the shop?" asked Jan. "The one with the gas mask in the window?"

Emmie shook her head sadly. "No," she replied, "we've been up and down the road it was on, both walking and on the bus, but it's not there." The road was blocked with some rubble from a damaged building but we eventually managed to get around from the other side to check.

"It must be the key to this, though," Stan piped up, "you said it was unusual for it to be there on your journey home from school and having a gas mask from the war must be significant. I'm guessing people in the future don't still carry gas masks?"

Emmie laughed – "No, thankfully not."

"We should try and help you find that shop," Stan suggested, "it's probably your best chance of getting home." He looked at Jan, whose face was very glum – "I know they're your friends and you probably don't want them to leave but we know this part of London pretty well between us and I think we should help. It might be in a different place now."

"You're right," Jan agreed in a small voice. "I'd hoped we might have a fun day together, but I guess we can still have fun searching for the shop."

Emmie smiled at Jan – "Thank you, that's really kind," she said. Then she looked at Stan – "How about we go to the factory and help you with that radio too? See if we can tune into a Polish station?"

Stan's face broke into a big grin – maybe today would finally be the day he got to hear some news from home...

22

The Polish Service

"We should approach this logically." Jan turned around to face the others as they walked down the road, away from the shelter house. "Let's start with Stan and I thinking about blue painted shops near where we live. Then we can decide where to look first."

Emmie smiled as Jan spoke – he was really coming out of his shell now; nothing like the timid boy they'd met on that second night in the crowded Tube station.

"I think there's a blue or grey shop along from the library," suggested Stan. He was keen to help out and had done his fair share of walking the streets recently.

"Let's go there first," Jan said excitedly. "Come on!"

The others chuckled at his enthusiasm as they followed along behind – Jan almost breaking into a run on the pavement in front of them.

"Slow down, Jan!" called Jack after a moment, "we've got all day and you'll be tired out if we run everywhere."

"Sorry..." Jan slowed down but chattered on

animatedly. He rattled off a whole list of shops which he thought were blue but couldn't be sure. The one which stuck in his mind, though, was not far from the paint factory.

"Maybe we can check that one out later?" suggested Emmie. "We said we'd help Stan with his radio so we can do them both together."

They approached the library — it was situated near the Gardens and sat a little way back from the road, behind a low wall. As they'd noticed previously, this was another building where the railings had been removed earlier in the war.

"Where's the shop?" asked Jack, looking around.

"Just around the corner from the library." Stan pointed in front of them, long thin finger outstretched. He led the way past the library entrance and turned right, indicating the blue painted façade.

"Is this it?" Emmie looked at Jack and frowned — there wasn't room for a bus to drive past this shop. "What do you think it sells?" she asked.

They stared at the shop, which had no discernible signage and darkened, empty windows. Jack walked up to the door and tried the handle. It was locked. "Looks closed," he remarked unnecessarily. He peered through the glazed door — "Oh look, there's a notice inside, propped up on a chair." Cupping his hands around his eyes to see better, he began to read —

Closed for the duration. "The duration of what?" he wondered aloud.

"The war, silly!" Emmie said, wondering how someone so bright could sometimes ask such simple questions. "Whatever they were selling, they aren't now. It can't be our shop."

They spent the rest of the morning in a fun, but ultimately fruitless, walk around the streets of Bethnal Green. There were a number of blue shops, in a surprising range of shades, but none were remotely right. They'd looked at a fishmonger, a bric-a-brac shop and a greengrocer, as well as several more empty units, and now the ideas were beginning to dry up.

"I think we've done this the wrong way," volunteered Stan who, up to that point, had been rather quiet - in direct contrast to Jan's bubbly excitement. "You said you'd seen the shop on your bus journey home – have we walked along that route yet?"

"No... But we did walk along there the other day," replied Jack. He reiterated the story about trying to get on the bus and not having any money, then how they'd walked along the road to try and spot the shop. "We walked for a good few minutes along the road from the bus stop, but nothing..." he finished.

"We should go there anyway, walk a bit further maybe?" Stan persisted. "You might not have gone far enough. Anyway, we've nothing else to try." He walked ahead, with Jack giving directions.

"It's under the big railway bridge, just along Bethnal Green Road," he explained. As they reached the bridge, they found that the rubble had been cleared and the road was open once again. "This looks more promising," Jack said excitedly. They got to the bus stop and Stan asked where their school was. "About a mile further along the road," Jack pointed ahead of them.

"So, the bus comes straight along here?" Stan checked his understanding. When Jack nodded, he continued – "Let's go then – see what we can find over the next ten minutes or so."

They walked along the pavement, scanning each side of the road to no avail. There were a lot of shops, mixed in with tall three storey houses, but nothing with a blue front. Jack looked at Emmie, the same disappointed expression on his face which she had seen all too often of late. He didn't know how many more knock-backs he could take in their attempts to get home and was starting to disbelieve his own memory of events.

"School is just off to the right - in that road," Jack said quietly, indicating a small turning up ahead of them. "I guess we're not going to find the shop today..."

"Chin up," encouraged Emmie, "we've still got the one by the paint factory to check out" – though she didn't really believe it would be the right shop.

As the group walked south towards the paint factory, Emmie noticed how well Jan and Stan were getting on together. They clearly had an immediate bond, being both far from home and coming from Poland, but it was more than that – they seemed really comfortable in each other's company too.

Emmie elbowed Jack and discreetly pointed behind her at the pair. As Jack snatched a look over his shoulder, he saw them chatting animatedly together, oblivious to everything around them. "That's nice to see," he said quietly. "Jan isn't that confident and he's going to need a friend when we go home."

"If we go home…" replied Emmie.

Jack looked at her – "Don't be down. We'll find a way to get back – probably when we're least expecting to."

"Do you really think so?" Emmie's furrowed brow told him that she wasn't so sure. In truth, nor was he, but what else could they do except hope? It seemed like the whole of London in 1940 was built on hope, so a little more wouldn't matter surely.

Jack reached over and gave Emmie's shoulder a squeeze – "It'll be alright, you'll see."

They came to a road junction and crossed – the streets were quiet today and there was little traffic. Saturdays in wartime didn't seem that busy – Emmie remembered learning at school that factories and other businesses worked at weekends to keep up and that curtailed the amount of leisure time that people had.

"Is it always this quiet at the weekend?" she asked Jan. "Jan?" she repeated after a pause, smiling as he was obviously still deep in conversation with Stan.

"Uh, sorry - what did you say?" replied Jan, surprised and slightly distracted still.

"I asked if it was usually this quiet on a Saturday," Emmie explained. "I figured people are working more to help with the war effort."

"I think so – our neighbour works at the docks and he's certainly out early on a Saturday, like the rest of the week." Jan smiled and turned back to his discussion with Stan.

"Do you think this shop near the paint factory is going to be any help?" Jack said to Emmie.

"To be honest, no," came the reply. "I think the way back must be connected to the bus route somehow – we just need to work out how."

They passed another row of houses – it must have been the hundredth that day, or so it felt – and arrived at the road junction ahead of the railway bridge. This was where they had first seen Stan ducking through the fence into the factory.

"Where's that shop you thought was near the factory?" Jack asked Jan.

"Oh, I think it's back there," Jan replied, pointing to a side road behind them. "Sorry..." The other three let out pretend groans and rolled their eyes. As they turned to retrace their steps, Emmie asked what kind of shop it was.

"Hairdressers," Jan quickly responded without thinking further about it.

"Oh, well that's definitely not right," Emmie turned back again. "Let's save ourselves a trip." She led them back to the factory fence and wriggled through the gap.

As they reached the factory building, Stan felt a rush of excitement. He had worked for weeks to collect the parts he needed for the radio, then cautiously carried them here and assembled them. The first time he had tried to use it was a mix of elation at hearing the static, then intense disappointment as he realised he couldn't find any stations to tune into.

Each subsequent visit was a mix of nervous anticipation and hope that the radio was still there, untouched. It had felt like a fairly safe location to leave it in as the buildings looked more dangerous and dilapidated than they actually were. He had also never seen anyone else on the site, until the other day when he'd spotted Emmie, Jack and Jan as he was leaving.

They passed through the doorway and walked amongst the machinery, heading for the radio at the foot of the staircase. In places, there were puddles on the factory floor from the rain the previous day and they had to walk round a few of the larger ones to avoid getting wet shoes.

"It's still there!" said Stan - joyfully rushing over to his precious creation. He crouched down in front of the radio and began to carefully adjust it. As the others gathered around him and watched, they saw him gently moving the pencil lead around on the razor blade.

"What's he doing that for?" asked Jack, looking a little confused.

"Shh!" hissed Stan, "I've got something…" He screwed his face up tightly in concentration – his ear close to the tin lid and nail arrangement. Suddenly, he sat back with a big grin on his face – "It works!"

"Brilliant!" announced Jan, "well done Stan."

"It was just some music," Stan explained, "and it was really quiet - but it works."

"How do you tune it?" asked Jack, eager to understand more.

"You move the pencil lead around on the razor

blade to find different stations," Stan told him. "I can't quite remember why that works, but it's what the magazine said to do."

"Have another go?" encouraged Jan. In truth, he was as excited as Stan at the prospect of hearing Polish voices again.

Stan bent over the radio once more and a hush descended as Jan, Emmie and Jack watched him intently. He placed his ear close to the tin lid again and slowly circled the pencil lead around, tracing patterns all over the blade. Back and forth he went, occasionally moving his ear even closer when the static gave way to mumbled conversation.

"I don't think the aerial is long enough still," he said quietly, though he didn't move from his position. Jack slowly stepped back and climbed up the metal staircase, taking care not to make too much noise. At the top, he unhooked the wire from the wall and looked about for somewhere higher to attach it. His eyes settled on one of the broken skylights – he could probably just about reach it if he put a chair on one of the desks and stood on his tiptoes.

Emmie noticed what he was doing and hissed up at him – "Be careful!" He grinned down at her, raised his thumb and climbed onto the chair. As he stretched up and jammed the end of the wire into the window frame, he heard a shout of excitement below him. Scrambling down from the desk and taking the stairs two at a time, Jack was surprised when he reached the bottom to find everyone apparently in tears.

Looking closer, he could see that Stan was smiling broadly, though tears were pouring down his face and leaving grubby marks on his cheeks. Emmie was hugging Jan, and both had tears in their eyes. "What did I miss?" he asked.

Stan looked up at him, wiping the tears from his face. "The BBC Polish Service. It was like being back home."

23

Friendship

"So, it worked then?" asked Jack. "You managed to hear some voices from home?"

Stan was grinning wildly - his streaked face at odds with his happy expression. "Polish voices," he said, "but I think they broadcast from England." At the beginning of the war, he recalled being told that the BBC had started a Polish language station for the benefit of the large number of Poles who were arriving in Britain, and also in order that those still in Europe could hear unbiased reporting. "Thank you for fixing the aerial," he said to Jack – "you must have got it high enough for the signal."

"What were they talking about?" Emmie turned to Stan, giving him an encouraging smile.

"Umm…" Stan realised that, in his excitement, he hadn't actually listened to what the voices were saying. He bent his head back down to the radio and the others fell silent. After a few moments of concentration, he looked back up again. "They are talking about Polish pilots in the RAF – there are many of them."

Jan, who had enjoyed better access to the news lately than Stan seemed to have, joined in. "There are several squadrons of Polish pilots. They escaped from France with the British Army and are now fighting alongside the RAF." He went on to add that a lot of the Polish pilots were based at airfields around London.

"We might have seen them fighting off some of the raids overhead," suggested Jack. Jan agreed that this was quite likely – a proud expression on his face at the thought of his countrymen still helping the cause of freedom.

"You should try and find somewhere closer to keep your radio," Emmie said. "You don't want to be coming all the way over here every time you want to listen to the news."

Stan frowned and explained that he didn't think Mrs Smith would like him keeping it at her house and he wasn't sure where he could run the aerial wire either.

Jan, who appeared deep in thought, suddenly spoke – "Why don't you keep it at my house?" They all looked at him as he continued – "I think Mr Tubbs would like to see it – he likes clever inventions and you could tell him how you made it. Mama wouldn't mind either."

"Really?" Stan asked, grateful to have an unexpected option.

"Yes, definitely," replied Jan, "we could set it up in the outhouse in our yard — it's not very big but we could run the aerial wire up the side of the house and fix it to the drainpipe." He paused, looking very pleased with himself for suggesting all this.

Stan nodded — "Thank you, that would be good."

"I'd like to listen to the Polish news with you too," continued Jan, "it's been a long time since I've heard Polish voices either."

Emmie gave Jan a little smile — she was pleased to see him getting on so well with Stan. They hadn't been sure about the older boy initially, but it seemed that he would be a good friend for Jan.

"Shall we help you pack it up?" asked Jack. Without waiting for an answer, he bounded up the stairs and climbed back onto the desk where he'd reached the skylight earlier. As he stretched to unhook the wire, he felt the chair wobble beneath him. He froze, then gently shifted his weight slightly more to the centre, in an effort to better balance it. Holding his breath, he carefully knelt on the chair seat and clambered back down onto the desk, wire in hand. Daring to breathe again, he started to coil the wire up, following it back down the steps as he did.

As he reached the bottom, Stan was gently sliding the radio, still mounted on the wooden base, into Jan's satchel. "Do you want me to carry it?" he asked.

Jan's face turned a little pink – "It's ok, I can manage." He felt proud to be carrying his friend's treasured possession. Jack handed him the coil of wire and he slipped it in alongside the radio. "Are we ready to go?" he asked.

Emmie took a look around the factory floor – nothing looked out of place, and they hadn't left anything behind. "Yes – all good."

They filed back towards the door, passing the giant mixing machines and the larger puddles. "Do you think we'll be back?" whispered Jack to Emmie.

"Probably not," came the reply. "It sounds like Stan has a new place to hang out, which is great news."

Crunching across the gravel which led to the fence, Stan suddenly felt an immense warmth towards these children who had shown him such kindness. As they reached the fence, he turned to face them – "This has been the best day ever." His eyes welled up for the second time that afternoon and Emmie put a friendly arm round him.

"You're welcome," she said, "you've not had the best experience of our country so far and I hope it's better from now on."

Stan hugged her back and wiped his eyes, then feeling slightly awkward at his rush of emotion, led the way through the fence and back onto the pavement.

A little while later, as they approached Jan's house, Stan put his hand on his new friend's arm. "Are you sure they won't mind me coming in?" He wasn't used to hospitality being offered in his direction.

"Of course they won't!" Jan reassured him. Mama was always asking him about his friends at school and whether he wanted to invite them round for tea. He felt sure she would be excited to meet the boy.

Stan looked nervous as they stopped outside the house. "If you're sure," he said hesitantly.

"Ok, we'll leave you to it," Jack announced. He was tired after the day's exertions and wanted a lie down.

"Shall we see you tomorrow?" asked Emmie. "It's Sunday – we could have a picnic and work out what to do next. Maybe we can walk the bus route one last time – I'm not quite sure what to do other than that?"

"Yes please," replied Jan and Stan together.

"Ok – meet us outside the house in the morning then? Bye!" With that, Jack and Emmie walked off down the road, turning to wave as they went round the corner and seeing that Jan and Stan had already disappeared inside.

Jan pushed the front door open and called into the house as he entered - "I'm home." He held the door for Stan and then shut it carefully, just as Mama came bustling through from the kitchen.

"Oh, hello!" she said, noticing Stan standing awkwardly in the hallway. "Who's this then, Jan? A friend from school?"

"Yes, kind of," replied Jan, "we've been playing together."

"I'm Stan," the boy said nervously.

"Ah - you're Polish too," observed Mama, smiling warmly at him. "Nice to meet you, Stan. Any friend of Jan's is welcome in our house." She noticed the bulging satchel – "What have you got stuffed in there, Jan?"

"It's a radio," explained Jan, "Stan built it himself." He edged the corner out of the bag to show her.

"Did he now?" came a new voice – it was old Mr Tubbs, who had come shuffling out of the sitting room to see what was going on. "Does it work?"

Stan nodded – "It does, and we managed to hear the BBC Polish Service on it earlier."

"Oh, that must have been lovely," Mama chipped in, "Jan talks about Poland a lot – you must both miss it terribly."

Jan explained that Stan had come to England on the Kindertransport, just like he had the previous summer. He went on to say that he hadn't found a host family straight away so had been in the transit camp for a few weeks.

"You poor thing," Mama told Stan, "Jan said it used to be a holiday camp but I don't suppose being shut up in it was much like a holiday."

Mr Tubbs interrupted at this point – "Enough of all that – can I see this radio?"

"You'd better set it out on the kitchen table," Mama offered, and then retreated to put the kettle on.

Jan carefully carried his satchel into the kitchen – Stan and Mr Tubbs following. He set the bag down on the table and slid out the radio. "All yours," he said to Stan.

Stan spent a happy 10 minutes explaining how he'd made the radio from left over bits that he'd found, based on the magazine article. Mr Tubbs was very impressed at his ingenuity and kept saying over and over how clever Stan was. "Can we listen to it then?" he asked.

Stan pulled the coil of wire out of the satchel – "We'll need to hang this from somewhere high."

"Go upstairs and open the back window – you'll be able to reach the drainpipe and you can fasten it to that," suggested Mr Tubbs. No sooner had the words left his mouth than Jan was out of the room and heading up the stairs. There was a creaking noise from the window and then Stan heard Jan shout something to him.

"What was that?" he asked, walking to the bottom of the stairs.

"I said – go outside and catch this," came the voice from the rear bedroom. Stan went to the back door, opened it and stepped into the yard. A chicken's cluck made him jump, before he realised what it was and then looked up at Jan leaning out of the window. In his hand was the coil of wire and, without a further word, Jan dropped it in Stan's direction. Stan just about managed to catch the unravelling coil and looked up to see Mr Tubbs beckoning through the kitchen window. He slid the window open and passed the depleted coil through it.

Returning to the kitchen, Stan fastened the end of the wire onto his radio board and stood back. "It's ready now," he explained.

"One thing that's puzzling me," Mr Tubbs admitted, "is how you hear anything. There's no earphones, are there?"

"I made a speaker." Stan was growing in confidence now and pointed to the tin lid arrangement. He explained that he'd had to make everything because he had no money for proper radio parts, and that the speaker was basically some nails, bound tightly together, with the lid from a tin balanced on top. "It works on vibrations," he finished.

"Well I never," Mr Tubbs was almost speechless –

not something which happened often.

Stan leaned over the radio and began to adjust it. To start with, there was the faint hiss of static, which then gave way to an instantly recognisable big band tune. Mr Tubbs moved his head closer and then began to hum along with the song. "That's amazing," he said after a while, "and to think you did that all by yourself. Well done, lad."

Stan's face went bright red with a mix of embarrassment and pride, just as Mama turned around and placed hot mugs of tea in front of them. "I tell you Stan," she announced, "it's a rare thing that someone gets praise like that from Mr Tubbs." This did nothing to calm the colour of Stan's cheeks, but did add a shy smile to his face.

"Stan was wondering if he could keep the radio here," asked Jan. "I'd really like to listen to the Polish news with him sometimes, and his host probably won't like him taking it home."

"Of course he can," Mama said with a beaming grin. She was so pleased that Jan had brought a friend home that he could probably have asked for almost anything at that point. Turning to Stan, she asked, "Where do you live then?"

"Stepney," he replied, "not too far away."

Mama looked outside – "Much as I don't want to send you away, you might want to think about getting back. It's clear tonight, so there'll probably be a raid and you don't want to get caught out in it."

Stan nodded – he ought to go home tonight, especially as he hadn't been back the night before.

"Come back in the morning?" suggested Jan, "we can meet the others then." Over his shoulder, Mama's grin got even bigger – others? – that meant Jan had even more friends for her to meet.

Stan headed to the door – "Thank you," he said to Mama and Mr Tubbs. As he left, the warm feeling from earlier returned, and he realised this was the first time in ages that he was going home happy.

The Last Bus

Jack woke up with a start. He was sure he'd heard a strange, rumbling sort of noise outside but couldn't be totally sure that he wasn't dreaming. He lifted his head up, straining to listen to what was going on outside the shelter. There it was again – definitely a rumbling and he hadn't imagined it. He quietly slipped down from the bunk and peered around the blackout curtain, trying not to disturb Emmie who was clearly still asleep.

The sight which greeted him chilled his blood. There were several lorries parked in the street outside the house and workmen were putting a fence up along the pavement. As he watched, an excavator rumbled off the back of one of the lorries and started to crawl towards the largest pile of rubble. Alarmed, he dropped the curtain and turned to wake Emmie.

"It's ok, I'm awake..." she said sleepily, as he turned around. "What's going on out there?"

"I think they're clearing the site," Jack explained, a mournful expression on his face.

"Oh no!" Emmie put her hands to her face in horror. "What does that mean for us?" Jack didn't get a chance to reply as, at that moment, a group of workmen fanned out noisily to check the remaining structures in the garden. Instead, he grabbed his bag, pulled her by the arm and they slipped out of the shelter, heading for the outbuilding. They ran around it and crouched down behind the woodpile at the rear. As they watched, one of the workmen tugged the curtain of the shelter open, looked inside and then shouted 'all clear'.

Jack and Emmie breathed a sigh of relief which turned out to be very short-lived, as another workman rounded the outbuilding and spotted them hiding. "What are you doing here?!" he asked. "You need to go now – this place is too dangerous for kids." Jack started to say something, but the man cut him off. "No buts, sonny, boss's orders."

Jack and Emmie grabbed their bags and turned to look back at their temporary home as they walked slowly across the lawn – what would they do now?

"Let these kids through," called the workman from behind them as they reached the new fence. A pair of hands moved one of the panels aside and they slipped through.

"Go on – scarper!" said the voice that belonged to the hands. This was probably the boss – he wore a different coloured set of overalls and had a sheaf of papers protruding from his pocket. Jack and Emmie did the only thing they could and walked reluctantly off down the road, skirting the lorries and piles of equipment strewn along the pavement.

"We can't go too far – Jan and Stan were coming to meet us," Emmie reminded Jack, as they walked around the first bend in the road.

"Good point," he replied, suggesting that they sat down on a wall to wait for the others.

About half an hour later, after watching the first lorryloads of rubble get carted away down the road, Jack spotted Jan and Stan coming towards them. He jumped up from the wall and started waving.

"What are you doing out here?" asked Jan. He noticed Emmie's expression, "Are you ok?" he added.

"They're clearing the house," Emmie said sadly. "Take a look around the corner."

Jan ran around the bend in the road and came back looking shocked. "Is the shelter gone too?"

"Not yet, but the workmen told us to leave as it wasn't safe," Jack joined in.

"What will you do now?" asked Stan. He'd been looking forward to today and now it seemed to have taken a downward turn.

"Let's have the picnic and then try to work out a

plan." Jack was trying put a brave face on things for his own benefit, as much as everyone else's. It was looking to be a nice, sunny day and talking about what to do next as a group would be helpful.

"Ok – shall we go to the Gardens?" Jan used to like running around on the wide expanse of grass, though there was a lot less of that these days now most space had been turned over to growing vegetables.

Everyone nodded in agreement and the group made their way along the road towards Bethnal Green Gardens. When they arrived the side gate was still shut, so they carried on round to the Tube station entrance, where the main gate was situated. They could see the WVS van was parked outside the station – a queue of people already formed and waiting for a hot drink and some bread. Jack suggested they join the queue as he and Emmie hadn't eaten that morning yet.

"Mmm, that's better," Emmie said through a mouthful of bread a few minutes later. "Food always tastes so good when you're hungry!" Jack mumbled his agreement as they wandered over to re-join Stan and Jan, who had been waiting inside the entrance to the Gardens.

"Let's find a good spot to sit down?" Jan ran ahead excitedly, looking for some grass in amongst the growing plots.

As they followed, Jack pointed to a rhododendron bush – "That's the bush we hid from the policeman behind, isn't it?" Emmie laughed in agreement and recounted the story to Stan, who was walking alongside them.

Jan was up ahead waving and pointing – as they reached him, they could see that there was a small, grassed area nearby which would be perfect for their picnic. It was sheltered on one side by trees and was facing into the warming, autumn sun.

They sat and chatted – Emmie interested in how Stan's meeting with Mama had gone the previous evening, and Jan eager to provide every last detail. "So, will you go around to listen to the radio often?" she asked Stan.

"I hope so," he answered, "Jan's family were very nice to me, and it was better than hiding out in that draughty factory."

"What shall we do about the picnic food?" Jan asked. "I should have brought something from home."

Jack put his hand into his pocket and brought out the remaining coins. "We can go and buy some food with this," he said. Turning to Emmie, he added sadly – "Not like we need it for the bus now…" Any optimism that he may previously have had was lost when they were forced to leave the shelter.

"We'll find our way home somehow – you'll see," she replied, putting her hand on his arm. She too was struggling to find any positives from their newest predicament. "I'm happy to spend it though."

"Want to come to the shop with me?" Jack asked Stan. He knew that he'd misjudged the boy to begin with and was keen to show his change of attitude.

Stan smiled with pleasure at this suggestion – "Oh, yes please."

A little while later, the two boys returned with their arms full of provisions. There were bottles of lemonade, bread rolls, a tin of Spam and a crunchy apple each. "We spent it all, but we'll be full after this lot," Jack said happily.

They arranged the food in the middle of their circle and dug in hungrily. It was quiet for the first time that morning as they concentrated on eating, licking their lips happily when they had eventually finished.

Jack asked Jan and Stan to tell them a bit more about the Polish pilots who were flying with the RAF. He was curious to learn about events that people felt a personal connection to, as it always made them seem more interesting. "Of course, Polish pilots are the bravest in the world," boasted Jan, whose parents had taken him to watch air displays in Poland before the war.

The others chuckled as Jan said this – he was very proud of being Polish and it had given him a real lift hearing news from home, especially as some of it had been about Polish pilots in England.

As the day wore on, thoughts returned to where Jack and Emmie would spend that night safely. Jan tried to convince them that Mama wouldn't mind two more house guests, but Emmie knew this would be a big ask in a small house. "I guess we'll just have to try the Tube station again..." she concluded reluctantly. "We might need to get used to it, after all."

They got up and decided to have a wander together, before making a final decision. As they walked back through the Gardens towards the Tube station entrance, Jack looked up at the sky. "Looks like we're due some more rain." He thought back to that first time they'd entered the station to shelter from a storm, and how long ago it seemed now. In reality, it had only been a few days but felt much longer.

As they passed the entrance, Emmie noticed the familiar, unwashed smell emanating from inside. She shuddered a little – it wasn't somewhere she was looking forward to going back to.

They crossed the road and passed by the pub on the other side of the junction, before heading under the railway bridge. "This is where your bus stop was, isn't it?" asked Stan thoughtfully. Jack and Emmie shut their eyes, remembering the flash as they'd stepped off the bus and how they'd thought little of it at the time.

As they walked further, Jack spotted something in the distance and then blinked – looking harder this time. "Wait here a minute," he said and, without a further word, sprinted off down the pavement. The others watched with a mixture of shock and surprise as he came to a halt a few hundred metres along the pavement and then waved frantically at them.

Emmie looked at Jan and Stan, said "Guess we'd better go then," and started to walk towards Jack. As they got closer, they could see that he was pointing across the road and as Emmie followed his gaze, she stopped dead in her tracks.

It was the blue shop. Not just any blue shop but the actual blue-fronted antique shop they'd seen from the bus window. The mannequin with the long dark coat and the gas mask was still there, looking out at them. It definitely hadn't been there before, had it? Where had it reappeared from?

Emmie tried to speak but couldn't. Jan and Stan stared at her and slowly realised the cause of her reaction. "Is that the shop?" Stan asked. Emmie nodded, tears pricking at her eyes. What did this mean? Were they going to be able to get home after all?

"You should go inside and see what you can find out," suggested Jan. Jack had walked the short distance back to them by this point and agreed. Looking left and right, they crossed the road and approached the shop. It had a large window on the right, with a partly glazed door alongside. There was no signage, which was a bit odd, and it didn't look open.

Jack reached for the door handle and tried to turn it. Nothing. The shop was shut. "What do we do now?" he asked Emmie – the earlier elation quickly disappearing.

"I really don't know," she said dejectedly. The shop definitely meant something, and it hadn't been there before, but what part did it play in getting them home?

"Hey, look!" Jan's shout got their attention and, to everyone's surprise, they observed a red double decker bus making its way slowly along the road.

Jack looked at Emmie – "This has got to mean something," he said, the excitement returning in his voice. They quickly crossed the road again and stood by the nearby bus stop.

"We haven't got any money left," Emmie sighed.

"We've got to try it anyway – this is too good to pass up," he replied.

As the bus slowed, they could see that there was no conductor standing on the rear step. "That's fate," declared Jack, "this could be it!" He and Emmie turned to say goodbye to Jan and Stan.

"Go, go!" said Stan, "you're right – you have to try."

Jack and Emmie stepped onto the bus and sat down by the window. There was no-one else on board, except for the driver. They waved to Jan and Stan as the bus pulled away, both feeling quite emotional.

All of a sudden, the sky darkened, and rain started to fall heavily, drumming on the roof of the bus. There was a bright burst of lightning, followed by a loud clap of thunder and, when Jack looked back out of the window, Jan and Stan were gone. As he stared harder through the streaming rain, he could see that the road was now busy, and the cars looked modern. He glanced down at his seat and noticed that it was different – the brown leather having given way to a bold, check fabric.

Emmie had been staring out of the window too and Jack saw that her mouth was wide open in shock as the realisation hit her. "I think we're back..." she said slowly - the confused expression on her face giving way to a cautious smile.

Jack scratched his head – could it actually be true? He'd spent a lot of time over the past few days almost unable to believe his eyes and this was no different. It definitely looked like the present day – but was it really? "Are you sure?" he whispered, reluctant to open himself up to further disappointment.

"100%," replied Emmie, "look – there's the paper shop. No rubble in sight. I don't know what just happened but we're home – that's the main thing."

Jack looked down at his watch and noticed it still said 4:35. Suddenly, the war-damaged streets of the capital felt a lifetime away. Had they really been there or was this just some kind of weird dream?

He shrugged with confusion and then, feeling something in his pocket, Jack put a hand in and pulled out a small coin. It was copper coloured and, as he turned it over, he read the date stamped on it. "1940," he said, "I guess it was real after all..."

For The Curious...

Kindertransport

The Kindertransport (which is German for 'children's transport') was a rescue mission which took place over 9 months, starting in December 1938. The purpose was to help children in countries threatened by or under German occupation get to safety in the lead up to the Second World War.

In the end, the United Kingdom took in nearly 10,000 children from Germany, Austria, Czechoslovakia, Poland and the Free City of Danzig (a city state between Germany and Poland which existed between 1920 and 1939). Most of the children rescued were Jewish and, sadly, many of them were the only members of their families to survive the Holocaust.

Bethnal Green Tube Station Disaster

The Tube station did exist during the period Jack and Emmie explore in the book and it was used as an air-raid shelter at the time.

Sadly, on 3rd March 1943, 173 people, including 62 children, were killed in a crush whilst trying to enter the shelter during an air-raid. This is believed to be the largest loss of civilian life in the United Kingdom during the Second World War.

At the time, the disaster was kept quiet and not widely reported, for fear of encouraging further raids. A secret investigation was held and determined that the cause had been panic amongst the people trying to get into the shelter after hearing anti-aircraft rockets being fired from a nearby park.

In 2017, more than 74 years after the disaster, a public memorial sculpture was unveiled outside Bethnal Green Tube station to remember those who lost their lives in this tragic accident.

Can You Really Make a Radio Yourself?

Yes, you can! In the Second World War, soldiers often used to make 'foxhole' radios out of everyday material.

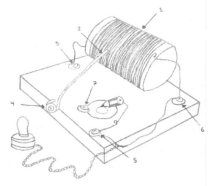

1 Copper wire wrapped around cardboard tube
2 Coat hanger wire bent to touch coil
3 Connect to aerial – long wire hung outside
4 Movement allows tuning of radio
5 Safety pin inserted into end of pencil
6 Connect to water pipe to create an earth
7 Washer – move pencil around to get best signal

The most important thing here is that, unlike Stan, we're not going to use a razor blade. Soldiers used razor blades because they were available, and the type of metal used helped with the radio signal. Any rusty piece of metal will work the same way – we will be using a rusty washer instead.

Assemble your radio as shown above – the earphone can be bought from any electronics supplier. The radio does not require any power and will pick up stations broadcast on medium wave (or AM), so you may have differing results depending on where you live.

For further information, search the Internet for 'foxhole radio' – there are some great resources out there.

About The Author

Glen Blackwell lives in Suffolk, England. He has a career in finance and *The Blitz Bus* is his second book. Inspired by bedtime reading with his 3 daughters, Glen loves to bring stories to life for young readers.

Glen would love to hear what you thought about *The Blitz Bus* – please contact him as below:

www.glenblackwell.com

Facebook.com/glenblackwellauthor

Twitter: @gblackwellbooks

Instagram: @gblackwellbooks

Alternatively, please leave a review on Amazon or your favourite online bookstore so that other readers can see what you thought.

Thank you!

Readers' Club

It would be great if you would like to join Glen's Readers' Club. Sign up to receive a free eBook at **www.glenblackwell.com/readersclub**

You will also be the first to hear about Glen's new books and get the chance to become an advance reader for new titles.

If you are under 13 then please ask an adult to sign up for you.

Follow Glen

Facebook.com/glenblackwellauthor

Twitter: @gblackwellbooks

Instagram: @gblackwellbooks

Join Jack and Emmie's Next Adventure...

Printed in Great Britain
by Amazon

87021139R00133